The Value of Love

By: Tamond Cole

The Value of Love

The Value of Love

Chapter 1

"**O**h, somebody help me please!" Tiffany Tyler yelled at the top of her lungs. She was a young black female with a thick, curvy body.

She snuck into an abandoned apartment because she was in so much pain. Being only sixteen and a full nine months pregnant, she was all alone and didn't know what to do. It was dark and raining outside so she sat down on the apartment floor in the dark, wiggling and moaning in so much pain. She felt as if she was going into labor but she was so scared. This was her first child, and she was facing it all alone.

"Please, somebody, help me, please!" She yelled out as loud as she could. But no one came to help.

She stripped out all her clothes then laid on the floor naked. She grabbed her purse and felt around in it for no reason at all. The only things she had in her purse was a can of mace, a blade, and a box cutter for protection.

She stood up, picked up her shirt and panties off the floor and took them outside in the rain so they could get soaked with water. As she stood there naked, she looked around. No one was in sight. She stepped out in the rain to cool herself down. She went back into the apartment and laid on the floor in front of the open door to give herself a little light in the apartment from the streetlight.

She held her breath every time the pain got too harsh. She wiped her face with her wet panties to try to keep herself cool. The pain was so strong, and all types of fluids started running out of her from between her legs. She cried but it was a silent cry.

Then her mind flashed back to why she ran away from home in the first place. "Love" is what got her where she was. Opening up her legs to an older guy for the first time ever. She was so happy when she told him she was pregnant, but his response and actions after she told him made her feel low.

"Tiffany, are you crazy, girl? You are too young to be pregnant by me. You're only fifteen and I'm twenty. Your parents will put me in jail."

"Tony, I promise I won't tell my mom or dad that I'm pregnant," she said.

"They are going to find out, Tiffany, because you stay there."

"No, they won't. I'll just leave, Tony."

"What the hell do you mean leave?"

"I'll run away so you and I can be together with our baby."

"Tiffany, I still stay with my mom. So where are you going to go? Because you cannot stay here. I'm telling you, girl, that I do not want to go to jail."

So, to keep the man that she loves so much out of jail, she ran away and stayed in the streets which didn't do her any good because he still broke up with her three months ago. But to keep her promise to him she decided not to go to the hospital to have the baby. Plus, she felt that once she had the baby that her and Tony could work things out and get back together. She wanted a child, but she wanted Tony back more than anything.

She wiped her face with her wet panties again, then pushed and pushed to get the baby out of her. Then she noticed that when she pushed the pain kind of stopped. So, she pushed and kept pushing harder and harder until she felt a big snap in her private area. She screamed out loud from the pain that followed the snap, but she kept pushing and she was not giving up. Then, she felt herself opening up wide between her legs, and something other than blood, piss, and water started to come out of her. She shook from the pain, and not knowing what was going on, she pushed her hardest while biting down on her bottom lip and pulling her hair out. She pushed so hard that her bowels burst loose, and she shitted all over herself.

She felt like something wasn't right, because she started shaking and cramping up. All she knew to do was to keep pushing. She didn't want to die like this so she pushed and pushed until she felt a heavy little load hanging a little more than halfway out of her. She looked and carefully pulled the baby out of her while she pushed. Once she got the baby all the way out of her, she took several deep breaths. She could not believe that she just had a baby on her own.

She wiped her face off again with her panties. She smeared blood on her face not knowing blood was on her panties from her hands from when she pulled her baby out. She held her baby up just looking at it. Then she looked to see what sex the baby was. A little girl. She had just given birth. She moved the baby around trying to see why the baby was not moving. Then she looked at the cord that was attached to the baby and still stuck inside of her. She grabbed her blade and cut the cord as close as she could to the baby's belly button. She grabbed her wet shirt and started wiping her baby off. She cleaned the baby's ears, mouth, nose, eyes, and everything. Once her baby was clean, she smacked the baby on the butt like she had seen doctors do in so many movies.

She jumped and almost dropped her baby when the baby burst out crying. She was so happy the baby was okay; she could not stop smiling. She tried to get up but sat back down due to so much pain. "Shit!" She screamed out.

Then, she pushed, trying to get the egg sack out of her. She stopped pushing once she felt like all the after birth was out. Then she fought against all the pain and stood up. She stood in the doorway naked, holding a crying newborn baby. She placed the baby on the floor right in front of the apartment door so she could still see the baby while she stepped outside in the rain to clean herself up. Once she got done cleaning herself up, she just stood there in the rain, looking up so the raindrops could hit her in the face. She walked back into the apartment and got dressed. She put both of her socks in the crotch of her panties to hold the leakage from her throbbing vagina. She cleaned the apartment with her wife beater and rain water.

She wrapped her baby in her sweater. She only had on shoes, panties, jeans and a shirt. She did not want to put on the bra. She held her crying baby in her arms and left.

Soon as the rainwater hit the lil' baby, the baby stopped crying. She had her sweater wrapped around her baby tightly. She walked up to the apartment dumpster and said, "Lord, forgive me," because she knew that she could not keep the baby. She tossed her little newborn baby girl in the dumpster and walked away. She heard the lil' baby start back crying but she kept walking away with Tony on her mind, hoping that they could get back together now.

The loud thump from the baby hitting the bottom of the dumpster woke up Betty. Betty is a white female bum that has been sleeping behind the apartment dumpster for six months. She made that her home six months ago when she discovered that it's always food and good clothes in the dumpster. When she heard a baby crying, she got up and walked from under her tarp. The rain was cold and coming down fast. She looked into the dumpster and she could not believe it really was true.

She looked around to try and spot who could have and who in the hell would do something like this. But no one was around at all. So, she climbed into the dumpster and got the baby out. It has been so long since Betty held a little baby. Betty was thirty-eight with three of her own who were all eighteen or older. Once Betty got the baby under her tarp she lit up a candle so she could see the baby better. The baby stopped crying once it seen the light. Betty looked at the lil' cute, dark skinned baby girl. The baby was too dark to pass for Betty's baby. Betty just looked at the baby not knowing what to do. All she knew is that she needed some money. So, she sat and thought real hard on who she could sell this baby to. But no one came to her mind. She knew that she had to get rid of this lil' baby. She could not afford to take care of herself, so the baby was a burden. She blew out her candle and walked the lil' baby to the 7-Eleven store. She walked into the store and put the little baby down on the counter next to the cash register and walked out the store without saying one word.

"Hey, you're leaving your baby, lady!" The young white boy yelled from behind the counter trying to stop Betty, but she kept walking so he picked up the phone and called the cops and told them what had just happened.

The police came and took the little baby away.

Chapter 2

"**B**aby, I need your help with this for a second," Gina said to her husband Keith.

"Gina, why are you fooling around with that laptop when you know that we are pressed for time? Not only that, I thought we both agreed not to do any work this weekend. That we were just going to enjoy our vacation."

"You're right and I'm sorry, baby," Gina said and closed the laptop. "I really just want to make this sale. For some reason I'm a little nervous about this one." Gina, being a top-notch real estate agent, took pride in her work. She's a bright skinned, slim twenty-seven-year-old. Gina was beautiful and well advanced. Coming from nothing she fought hard to make it. The only thing she hated about her life was the fact that she could not have kids.

Gina and her husband Keith both had great jobs. Keith, a young black professor at the college UCF gives his wife anything she wants. They have a nice home, and together their yearly income is well over a $120,000. They both have the perfect life together.

"Gina, are you ready?" Keith yelled out from the other room.

He was okay with having no kids. But Gina wanted kids and she talked to him about adopting a child. He just didn't see the need or rush for a child. So, he told her they'd talk about that later.

"Yes, I'm waiting on you!" Gina yelled back.

Keith packed up all of their luggage into the oversized Yukon truck. Then they both left for their wonderful vacation.

Once they reached the lobby of the hotel, the receptionist asked for their ID and reservation. Soon as she looked at their paperwork she said, "Mrs. and Mr. Marshall. You two are going to love our underwater resort. So, please, follow me so you two can get ready."

They went forty feet underwater to their amazing hotel room. They were excited and mind-blown about all the things they were seeing underwater. They were only in their room for nine minutes and Gina already had taken twenty-three pictures. Their room was like a large aquarium. The only difference is that they were the fish. At fifteen hundred dollars a night. They rented the room for two nights to enjoy themselves.

"Baby, this is so romantic, and thank you," Gina said to Keith. She gave him a long hug followed by some sweet, soft kisses. Then they made love slowly but passionately.

Chapter 3

"Tiffany, what are you doing here?" Tony asked.

"I need to talk to you, Tony."

"I don't care what you need. I told you that you cannot just pop up to my house like this."

"Well, if it means anything to you, Tony, I had the baby last night."

"What? Are you serious?"

"Yes, I'm serious."

"Well, where is the baby?" Tony asked and stepped outside the house and closed the door.

"I don't have the baby, Tony."

"What do you mean you don't have the baby? You just said you had the baby last night."

"I did have the baby last night. But I got rid of it so we could be together."

"Tiffany, what the hell are you talking about?"

"Don't act like you care now, Tony. Because you told me that you didn't want anything to do with me anymore because of the baby."

"I didn't mean it like that, Tiffany. I just didn't want you around because you are too young. So, who did you give the baby to?"

"I threw the baby away, Tony, is that what you want to hear? You didn't want no part of our lives anyway."

"Tiffany, you are crazy. I don't care what I said. That don't mean throw a damn baby away. I'm going to get my keys so you can show me what you did with the baby."

Tiffany held her head down in full shame while Tony went into the house to get his car keys. Now she felt bad and stupid at the same time. The more she tried to please Tony the more she fucked up. Tony came out of the house and rushed her into the car. She told him to go to the Lee Apartments. He drove and she directed him to the exact dumpster. They both jumped out of the car and looked into the dumpster. The dumpster was completely empty. The garbage truck came through earlier and dumped it. Once Tiffany saw that the dumpster was empty, her heart dropped.

"Are you sure this is the right one?" Tony asked her.

"Yes, I'm sure. I know where I was."

"So, where the fuck is the baby?" Tony said with anger. Then he looked at Tiffany's stomach for the first time to make sure she was not lying.

"I don't know. She's gone. The whole dumpster is empty."

"She? So the baby was a girl?"

"Yes, I held her in my arms, and she was crying."

"You know what, Tiffany? You're a fucking murderer." He got back into his car and sped off. With so many bead thoughts about Tiffany he just shook his head.

Tiffany stood still and watched Tony leave. Looking until his car could not be seen anymore. Then she dropped down on her knees and cried. Tony's words crushed her feelings. Now she wished she would have kept her baby. She was so tired of living in the streets. She was only a kid

13

herself and she missed her parents. She wanted to go home. No more staying with friends, house to house. She was tired, lonely, and hungry. The streets were not for her. Chasing after Tony only made her make the wrong decisions that she wished she could take back right now. She thought about what her parents would think of her if she went back home after all this time. They never even knew she was pregnant. She was stuck in a hole that she dug herself. She had no one to turn to and crying was not helping. So, she got up and walked to a place that she once called home. To her parents' house.

Chapter 4

"**I** can't believe that I let you talk me into this, Gina."

"Well, that part is over with now, Keith. We are here now so stop complaining and come help me pick out one of these little cute baby girls."

Gina had finally talked Keith into adopting. They were at the Adopt a Kid Center, looking at the info book. Gina wanted a little girl so they could spoil her. It took her three months of talking to him about it before he decided that it's a good idea. Plus, since Gina could not have kids, he leaned on her side. She was the one who wanted a little girl, so he just agreed. If it was up to him, he would pick a little boy. But to keep Gina happy he would do anything, and to top it all off, deep down inside, he wanted a child anyway.

They both stopped on the photo of a dark skinned, cute, chubby baby girl. They read the story about her and understood why her name was Miracle. The little pretty baby girl was left on the counter of a 7-Eleven store the same night she was born. So, the foster care staff named her Miracle. The story about the lil' girl was so touching. The adoption center had no clue on who the parents were. It only stated a white female was seen dropping the baby off. They both agreed on picking Miracle as their choice. They also agreed on letting her keep the name Miracle.

Once all the paperwork was filed and signed, they took their lil' baby girl and went shopping. Happy and so excited about the little baby, Gina was so overjoyed. She could not stop thanking her husband for supporting what she wanted. They picked out Strawberry Shortcake for the baby logo. All the baby accessories were Strawberry Shortcake. They even decorated the baby room with Strawberry Shortcake. Gina picked that logo because she felt the little baby was so sweet. Gina could not stop holding the baby. Just looking into the baby's eyes made her feel like she has been missing the whole complete life of motherhood. Tears ran down her face out of hurt and happiness. Life is all about giving life and this is the closest she will ever get to giving a life. Now she felt that her and her husband were a complete family.

Two years later and little Miracle was walking and trying to talk. She was so fat and cute with chubby cheeks. All she did was smile and show off her four lil' teeth. She loved Gina more than anything. She didn't like being around Keith if Gina was home. So, it was plain to see that Gina spoiled the little girl. She even kept the lil' girl's fingers and toenails painted. They took so many pictures together. All through the house they had pictures posted up.

"Mama, I want that," Miracle said, pulling on Gina pants leg, pointing up at the ice cream cone Gina had just made.

Gina handed it to her, and she sat right down on the kitchen floor to eat it. Gina fixed another one for herself, then sat down on the kitchen floor beside Miracle to eat it. She laughed out loud when she saw Miracle catch a brain freeze. She laughed so hard that Miracle started laughing with her. She did everything Gina did, or at least she tried too

Keith walked into the house from a long, hard day at work. He was greeted by cold, sweet kisses by his wife and then his daughter. All he tasted was butter pecan ice cream. The only time Miracle really gave him any attention is when she saw Gina do it.

That's how she learned the words "I love you" so good and fast. By copying what Gina says to Keith. Miracle was so smart and she learned so easily. So, they both learned that they had to be careful about what they said around her. She picked up on things so fast that they could not believe it.

What was so strange to them was the fact that she did not like Gina or Keith's parents. But they still would keep her from time to time. Mostly when Keith and Gina had to work. They always would come by the house and sit, trying to get her used to them. When they say the word grandparents, Miracle runs up to Gina and holds on to her leg as tight as she could, while saying, "No! No! No," letting them both know that she did not want to go. Gina and Keith could not understand why because all her grandparents did was buy her stuff. It was so funny how she found out the difference between the words yes and no. When Gina was potty training her, Miracle ran into the living room and said, "Mama, bathroom."

Gina jumped up with a smile and said, "Yes."

So, Miracle pulled her clothes down right there in the living room and squatted to pee.

Gina yelled out, "No!"

Miracle looked at Gina with a frown on her face and said, "Bathroom, mama."

"Yes, go to the bathroom," Gina said.

Soon as Gina said that, Miracle smiled and squatted to pee again. But she kept looking at Gina who was running up to her.

"No! Miracle, don't you pee on my floor."

Miracle was so confused that she just started crying. Ever since that day she knew the words yes and no.

Chapter 5

Two years later, on Gina's 31st birthday, she was running late for work. She had just dropped Miracle off at Head Start. Since Keith gets off work before her, he picks Miracle up on his way home. Today was Gina's big day. She had one of the biggest sales to make.

Her appointment was in five minutes and she was about twenty minutes away. So she sped through traffic to try to make up at least seven minutes. As she drove, she picked up her phone and texted her secretary to tell her to inform her client that she will be about ten minutes late. She drove with one hand while she texted with the other. She drove so fast that now she was only thirteen minutes away and two minutes until her big appointment. She felt better that she thought of the idea to text her secretary. Now she could slow down since they knew she was going to be a little late. Soon as she pushed the send button on her cell phone to send the text, she looked up just in time to see that she sped straight through a red light. But it was way too late for her to hit the breaks.

A big Ram 1500 truck smashed right into her driver side. The impact was so hard that it flipped her car two times and it landed passenger side up. The truck did a three-sixty in the middle of the road three times before coming to a complete stop. Glass, rubber and car parts were all scattered out in the road. People stopped and got out of their vehicles to make sure that both drivers were okay.

Every person on the scene were on the phone with the police. The white man in the truck was alone. They helped him out of the truck and sat him down in the road.

He held onto the back of his neck saying, "I'm okay! I'm okay!"

Gina's car was upside ways with the passenger side up. The people that were helping had to climb onto the car and open the passenger side door. They had a hard time pulling Gina out the car. Once they got her out of the car, they found out that she was dead. She still had the look of shock on her face because her eyes and mouth were still wide open. So, she'd seen her death before she died. The man in the truck felt so bad. The police and the ambulance arrived and took over the scene.

Chapter 6

"Miss Tyler, I'm sorry, ma'am, but you are suffering from kidney failure. One of your kidneys are completely shot and the other one is not too much better. We were able to place a spring in your better kidney to keep you afloat. So, you will continue to feel a little pain in your side. Because the truth is that you need a kidney. So, we placed you on the donor list. But the list is at least a ten-year waiting period. So, if you stay away from drugs and maintain your health, you will be fine through the waiting period. Since you are not on the verge of death, we have placed you on the backend of the donor list. But please keep in mind that in the next seventeen years or so that your health will begin to be a major problem. So, in the meantime, please eat and stay healthy," the doctor told Tiffany and her parents then he walked out the room.

So now Tiffany knows what those harsh pains in her sides are since she had her baby. She was so happy that the doctor didn't say anything about her being infected with some type of disease. She was so scared of the pain that she kept feeling in her sides. So, she finally told her parents and they brought her to the hospital. She still has not told her parents about the baby. And being that it was four years ago, she hoped that the doctor would not be able to tell. She knew that if she told them that her parents would not forgive her for that.

She lied to them already to get back into their house. She told them that one day, when her friend girl left that the house where Tiffany had been staying, that the girl's daddy and brother tried to rape her. But she ran out the door before they had the chance to. She didn't even have to lie to her parents. Since she had left, they were so worried. They called the police station after they made the report once a week. They missed her so much. They prayed every night for their daughter. So, when she popped up on their doorstep, they were so happy to see her. They both thanked God for answering their prayers. All they wanted was to have their only child back home safe.

Tiffany felt so much better and she finally started to push Tony out of her mind but never her heart. She found out that Tony was now married with two kids from his wife, and that he worked for the city driving a school bus for kids. So he was doing good without her. Every day she wondered about how her life would be if she would have kept her baby. She felt so bad about killing her baby. But she kept her head up because she could not change the past. She said a special prayer for her dead baby every night. For some strange reason she felt like that was the ultimate sin that would never be forgiven. Even the bible stated that murder shall not be committed. Since that night, Tiffany gave her life to God. She also went back to school and got her G.E.D. She was so dedicated to the church that she even preached on Sundays. She found God to be the joy of her life. And she was so thankful to have such great parents.

The doctor came back into the room and handed Tiffany a prescription and told her to take the medication once daily on time, and that they were now good to go home.

Chapter 7

Keith, still stuck in a deep zone, was looking at his young wife laying in her casket waiting to be buried. He still could not believe the fact that his wife was gone. He was stuck looking at her for so long that his mom came up behind and hugged him. Trying to keep her son strong at his wife's funeral. She did not want him to break down and cry. Once she hugged him she brought him back out of his little trance. He looked around at everyone in the church. He had tears in his eyes that did not fall yet. As he looked around, he walked towards the door to leave. Until he locked eyes with lil' Miracle. She looked at him with so much concern and he knew she was scared. That is what stopped him in his tracks. Because he knew damn well that lil' girl did not have no idea of what was going on. And he also knew that she did not want to be with no one but him. He bent down on one knee and held his arms out towards her. She got up off the bench with Gina's parents and ran straight to him. He picked her up and walked out the church of his own wife's funeral. Everyone in the church just watched as he left. They knew he was crushed.

Soon as him and Miracle got into the car, she asked him, "Why mama not coming with us, daddy?"

"Because she is not here anymore."

"Yes, she is. I just seen her in there sleep, daddy," she said and pointed back at the church.

He looked at her then dropped his head and lied. "Yeah, mama is sleep right now," he said while driving off, thinking of what in the hell he could tell this lil' girl. She didn't know what death meant; she was too young. That was her first funeral and she didn't even know it. He knew that she was gone go crazy once she didn't see Gina later. She was already throwing fits for the past five days that Gina had been gone.

"I wake mama up, daddy."

"No, no, let mama sleep, okay?"

"Mama tired, daddy?"

"Yeah, mama tired right now. You want some ice cream?"

"Yeahhh! I want ice cream," she said.

He had to try to keep the lil' girl's mind off Gina. The good part about it right now is that she thought Gina was asleep. He could barely cope with Gina being gone. So, he knew that lil' Miracle would not be able to. He knew not that he had to put in a lot of time with Miracle to get her used to him. He really didn't know what to do. He was in deep thought as he drove to the ice cream shop. His mind was blank and his thoughts were so confusing. He didn't even pray anymore. He blamed God for everything. He figured why praise a killer?

He ordered Miracle her favorite butter pecan double-scoop ice cream cone. He made sure to get the candy sprinkled on top. All she did was smile with excitement looking at the ice cream as he handed it to her. He ordered a banana split for himself. Then they both sat down at a table outside and enjoyed their ice cream. Keith could not understand why him. His life just took a turn from great to disaster.

"Daddy, why mama sleep? I wake her up when we go back, daddy." She looked so happy eating her ice cream.

"No, Mircale, she has to stay there."

"So, why mama not coming home and sleep with me?"

"Miracle, listen to me," Keith said, being a little upset. "I'm about to teach you something about life. In life people have to go away. And mommy is gone away, okay?"

"When she coming back?" She asked with a sad look.

"She cannot come back. When you go away like mommy did, it means you die. So, mommy did not just go away, she died. When you die, you don't come back."

"Why mommy die, daddy?"

"Miracle, everybody has to die."

"Is die bad, daddy?"

"Yes, die means bad."

Miracle's lips turned upside down and her forehead wrinkled up. Keith knew she was about to cry; he knew that look too well. Miracle burst out crying, holding her ice cream cone dangling in her lil' right hand, looking Keith directly in his eyes as tears poured out of his.

Keith jumped up quickly and picked her up. She was so cute today. Dressed in her sky-blue Gucci Sunday dress with the light sky-blue barrettes in her hair. He took the ice cream cone out of her hand and laid it on the table right beside his own. He hugged her and she hugged him back tightly. Crying because she did not understand why Gina had to die.

"It's okay, Miracle," Keith kept telling her while he patted her on the back, walking to his car. He had no idea what to do with a crying little girl. So, he just held her tightly in his arms to show her love. He thought about taking her to his parents or Gina's parents. But then he thought against it. He put Miracle in her car seat. Then he just drove around not knowing where to go. So, he just drove and after a while of driving Miracle had cried herself to sleep.

Keith pulled up to his house. Parked the car and got Miracle out then went into the house. He felt so lonely and hurt that he just held Miracle in his arms while he cried silently. He stood in the middle of the living room looking at all the pictures. Miracle is the only thing he has left. So, he made up his mind to give her everything he could to keep her happy. The little girl was nothing but four years old and she already done had a rough life. She doesn't know nothing about her own life yet, and she is already losing out in someone else's life. Now how in the hell is he going to raise this little girl?

Keith laid Miracle down in his bed then walked into the kitchen and fixed him a straight shot of Hennessey. He downed that shot and fixed him another one. But drinking did not help the pain. So, he just sat down on the kitchen floor and cried. He cried out loud for the first time since

27

Gina died. He didn't even know how loud he was. It felt so good for him to cry that he woke up Miracle.

She walked into the kitchen, stopped and just stared at him. She was so surprised to see him sitting on the kitchen floor crying. He did not see her because he held his head down in his hands. She was scared because she had never seen Keith cry before. So, she just stood there and watched him cry. Then she walked up to Keith and touched his arm. He looked up in shock when he saw her. He did not want her to see him crying.

"Why you cry, daddy?" She asked him with a very concerned look on her face.

"I'm okay," Keith said and wiped his tears away.

"You miss mommy, daddy?"

"Yeah, I miss her a lot."

"I miss mommy, too."

"Well, it's going to be okay, Miracle. Anytime you want to talk, you can come talk to me, okay?"

"Okay, daddy. Can you fix me some food I want to eat?

"What do you want to eat?"

"Pizza!" She yelled out, jumping up and down with a big smile on her face.

So, Keith ordered pizza and hot wings. Once the pizza arrived, they both sat down at the dinner table ready to eat. He placed two slices of pizza and two hot wings on Miracle's plate. She waited until he poured soda in all both of their cups.

Miracle watched him until he tried to eat a slice of pizza.

"No, daddy, we got to say grace."

Keith put the pizza down and thought of Gina when she was teaching Miracle to say grace. And now Miracle has been stuck on that ever since. "Okay, Miracle, go ahead and say grace."

Miracle placed her hands in front of her together. Closed her eyes and bowed her head just like Gina taught her. "God is great, God is good. Let us thank you for our food. We bow our heads, we must be fed. We thank you for our daily bread. Amen!" She said and looked up at Keith.

"Thank you, Miracle."

"You can eat now, daddy," she said while grabbing a slice of pizza off her plate.

Chapter 8

At the age of seven Miracle was way more advanced than the average ten-year-old. Keith taught her so much and she learned so fast. With him being a professor, it was so easy for him to teach Miracle. All she wanted to do was learn. So that is how they spent most of their time. She was in the second grade. And the school board already had a meeting with Keith about placing her in the fourth grade. Because she was way too smart for her class. But Keith told them to give her a little more time so he can make sure that would be the right step for her. He did not want to make her uncomfortable by putting too much pressure on her even though he knew she was smart. He wanted to test her himself to be sure.

Since Gina's death they both do everything together. Keith can feel the love and he knows that they have grown much closer to each other. But the bad part about it is that since Gina's death neither of them have been to church. Keith still blamed God for taking Gina so he never went back and Miracle didn't either. His parents argued with him about that many times. But he still did not break. So, they tried to talk him into at least letting them take Miracle to church with them. She always said no. Something she did since she was young, and his parents did not like that. But Miracle always said grace and her prayers at night before she went to sleep. The only thing she loved more than Keith was school.

Now that she was older, she was starting to accept the fact that Gina was okay. Since Gina died, they took flowers to her grave once a month. Miracle had so many pictures in her room of her and Gina. Due to the fact that Gina died in the car wreck, the dude in the truck felt so bad that he decided not to sue. He only wanted his truck fixed. Gina had set up her life earnings to be split between Miracle and Keith. Miracle could not touch the money until she turned eighteen. So, she was well off already and didn't even know it. Plus, Keith had set up all his life earnings to go to her when he dies. After testing Miracle for the third time, he decided to let the school board place her up two grades. He talked to Miracle about it and she was happy and proud about it. He always told her that hard work pays off.

"Dad, I want to be smart enough to save people's lives."

"So, what do you want to be; a doctor or a surgeon?"

"Who saves more lives, dad?"

"I guess I'll have to say a surgeon does."

"Then that is what I want to be; a surgeon."

"Miracle, to be a surgeon it takes a lot of hard work and practice. Plus, you cannot be scared to perform."

"I won't be scared. Can you help me, dad?"

"Yes, I'll help you. But you got to keep up with your schoolwork and your good grades."

"I promise I will, dad."

"Okay, we got ourselves a deal, then. I'll get all the paperwork and books we will need to get started."

Once Miracle sets her mind at something, she always completes it. The main problem that Keith dealt with was when and how he was going to tell her the story about her life. How old is old enough to understand? He didn't know so he just waited.

Poor little Miracle went to school with the same hairstyle. A simple ponytail since Gina died. Because Keith did not know how to do hair. Then one day he made up his mind to start taking her to the hairdresser every two weeks. Whoever Miracle's mom was, she had to be beautiful because Miracle was a real beauty.

"Dad, I'm done with all my homework. Can I ride my bike?"

"Sure, you can. Just give me a minute to put these papers up so I can come watch you."

"Okay. Hurry up, dad." Miracle walked into her room.

Keith remembered the first night he had to give her a bath. She did not know how to clean her body at the age of four and he had to teach her. Now, that was hard and he felt so low. But she helped to make him out the parent that he is. She kept him on his toes. She was too damn smart.

He walked to her room to see if she was ready. When he walked into her room. She was trying to strap on her pink helmet. "Hey, cutie. You need some help?"

"I can do it by myself. Watch, dad."

He watched until she was finished. Then they walked into the garage and he let the garage door up. It was a nice, sunny day outside. Little kids were out playing everywhere just having fun. He helped her on her bike.

"Don't push me hard, dad."

"I won't. Are you ready?"

"Yeah!"

He gave her a soft push and she rode off smiling and laughing. She still had training wheels on her bike. But to him she still always seemed to be moving so fast.

"Don't go too far, Miracle!" he yelled out while walking out to the middle of the street so he could see her better.

Miracle was a good bike rider but she just did not know when to use her breaks. No matter how many times he tried to teach her, she just still would not use them.

Miracle road to the end of the street and was now turning around. She made sure that she stayed on the sidewalk just like he taught her. She was moving pretty fast on her way back. Then a blue Honda Prelude backed out and cut the sidewalk off right in front of her. Miracle crashed right into the side of the car and the car stopped.

Keith heard the sound of the impact from his house. "No! No!" He yelled out and took off running as fast as he could. By the time he got there, the driver was out of the car, on the ground, holding a little crying Miracle. Keith dropped to his knees and snatched Miracle out of the driver's arms. "Are you okay, baby? Where are you hurt?"

Just by Keith being there Miracle stopped crying. Keith asked Miracle the questions again. This time she answered by holding up her skinned-up knuckles to him and then she pointed at her skinned-up knees.

"I'm so sorry, sir. I did not see her," the driver of the car said.

"Well, you need to practice driving more, because you almost just killed my little girl," Keith said with so much anger that spit flew from his mouth. He stood up caring Miracle in his arms.

"Mister, I'm very sorry. I never meant to—"

Keith cut her words off in mid-sentence. "You need to learn how to watch where you're going before you kill someone, lady." Keith turned to leave, pulling her wrecked bike with his free hand. "Are you sure you're okay, Miracle?" He asked her as he carried her home.

"My hands and knees hurt, daddy."

"I'll make it feel better when we get home."

The driver of the car felt so bad. She really did not see that little girl. She wanted so badly to make sure that little girl was okay. She watched which house they went to so that later she could apologize and check on her. Keith walked into the garage and let the garage door down. He leaned Miracle's bike against the wall and walked into the house straight upstairs to the bathroom. He sat Miracle on the toilet lid and checked her over, making sure no bones were broken. The only thing that was wrong with her was she had skinned her knuckles and knees up. He took her helmet off and grabbed some iodine out of the medicine cabinet along with some q-tips. He cleaned her cuts and ran her bath water.

"You know when you get in that water your cuts are going to sting. But you've got to be a big girl and don't cry. Make sure you wash your cuts with soap. But not hard, okay? Wash them real soft."

"I'm a big girl, daddy. I won't cry," she said with a half-smile on her face.

"Good, I like to hear that. Once you are all dried off and dressed, call me back in here and I'll clean your cuts again. Then, you can come and help me cook dinner."

"Okay, I'm going to hurry up then."

Keith turned the water off. He stuck his hand into the water making sure it was not too hot. He walked out of the bathroom and closed the door. He went to Miracle's room and got her some night clothes and her lil house slippers. When he walked back to the bathroom door, he heard her groaning in pain as quietly as she could. That made his heart skip a beat. He leaned his head on the bathroom door. He was so scared when he seen that car back out in front of Miracle. He did not want anything to happen to this little girl. He loved Miracle with all his heart but he still wished that Gina was here to help him. He took a couple deep breaths and knocked on the bathroom door.

"Yes!" Miracle said.

"I got some night clothes and stuff for you."

"Well bring them in to me, dad. I'm naked."

Keith cracked the door open just enough to stick his hand and arm through. He felt around for the sink so he could drop the clothes on."

Miracle giggled. "I see you daddy. I know that's you."

"Yeah, it's me."

"Well open the door up then."

"No Miracle, I don't want to. You are old enough to have your own privacy. So from now on, do not let no one see you naked. Do you understand me?"

"Yes, dad."

He found the sink and dropped the clothes on it. Then, he closed the door and walked to his room. He sat on the bed and just stared at Gina's pictures. The pain he felt would never leave. It had been three years and he still felt crushed. Some things in life are meant for humans not to understand and death was one of them. Keith was stuck in his thoughts when heard Miracle yell, "I'm done, dad!"

He walked to the bathroom door and asked her.

"Are you dressed?

"Yes I'm dressed."

He opened the door, and she was dressed in her night gown sitting on the toilet stool looking at her cuts. He cleaned her cuts again but this time he put bandages over them.

"I don't like blood, dad."

"I know, Miracle. I don't like blood either."

"I don't want to bleed no more when I ride my bike."

"Well that means you got to be real careful, okay."

"Okay, dad."

"Now since you are all fixed up, let's go cook dinner."

They both went down to the kitchen together. Anything that was dealing with Miracle learning something, she was down with that. Plus, she always wanted to know how to cook.

Chapter 9

Tiffany got dressed for church. She got up a little early because she planned to make a special stop and drop the gift off that she had just bought and left in her car. She said her morning prayer and started humming the gospel song, Now Behold the Lamb while she got dressed. Her parents did not know why she was getting ready so early. Once she got ready, she got into her car and drove up to this big, nice house. She got out and looked around. She went and knocked on the door. It has been two whole days since she decided to come by this house. The front door opened up and she saw a very handsome black man. She looked at his ring finger and saw that he was married.

"Can I help you?" He asked her.

"Hello, my name is Tiffany Tyler, and I came to see if your little girl is okay."

"What do you mean to see if she is okay?"

"Well, two days ago, I accidentally backed my car up in front of her."

"Oh, that was you?" Keith said and looked her up and down.

He didn't recognize her because two days ago she did not look so stunning.

"So, is she okay?" Tiffany asked, breaking Keith's stare.

"Um yes, she is fine and thank you for asking."

"Is she home?"

"Yes."

"Can I see her and apologize to her please?"

"Well, hold on a second," Keith said and then called for Miracle to come here.

Miracle came to the door with a pencil in her hand. They were studying and watching surgeons videos. Soon as Tiffany saw her, she smiled.

"Hey Miracle, my name is Tiffany and I came to apologize for backing my car up in front of you two days ago."

"How do you know my name is Miracle?" She asked her.

"I just heard your dad call your name. I have a surprise for you."

"Why?" Miracle asked.

She have never liked other people since she was little. Plus, she was taught well not to talk to strangers.

"I'll be right back," Tiffany said and walked out to her car.

Keith and Miracle stood in the doorway waiting for her to return. She reappeared with a brand new bicycle for Miracle. She was struggling with the bike, so Keith stepped out and helped her with it. Then, told her thanks but no thanks. But Tiffany insisted on Miracle having the bike. So Keith finally gave in and agreed to let Miracle keep the bike.

Miracle's expressions told Tiffany and Keith that she was thankful for the bike. Before she even said thank you. Tiffany knew the little girl liked the bike. Tiffany looked at her watch and knew she had to be going.

"Is your wife home?" She asked because she had not seen her yet.

"Why is that any concern of yours?"

"I just wanted to be respectful and say hello to her mom."

"My wife passed three years ago."

"Oh, I'm so sorry to hear that, sir."

"It's okay and my name is Keith."

"Well it was nice to meet you, Keith. You and your daughter have a nice day. Hey, before I go, are you and your daughter coming to church?"

"No thank you on that, Tiffany."

Tiffany frowned her face up and asked, "Why?"

"We have our reasons, and I don't discuss my problems to strangers."

"Okay Keith, maybe you two will change your kind one day and give it a try. If you do, I'll be more than happy to introduce you to my church," she said then got into her car and drove off.

She waved goodbye to them. Keith carried the bike into the house, closed and locked the door behind him.

"So do you like this bike, Miracle?"

She looked at the bike and said, "Yes, but I don't want to ride it yet."

"Why not?"

"Because I might fall and hurt myself again. And I don't want to start bleeding again."

"I'll make a deal with you, Miracle. The next time you ride your bike, I'll be right behind you. So you will not fall or get hurt."

"Okay daddy, but I still got homework to do first."

"That was nice of that lady Tiffany to buy you a bike. But that do not mean that she is your friend."

"I know that, dad."

He grabbed Miracle, held her down and tickled her until she laughed so hard and had to take a deep breath. Once she was ready, they went back to studying.

"Miracle, why do you want to help save people?"

"So people will not have to die like Gina did."

"Look at me," he said. "You cannot stop that. Everybody has to die one day."

"But you told me that surgeons save lives."

"They do sweety but understand this, we all will have to die one day and can't no surgeon stop that."

"Why daddy," she asked, looking up from her paperwork.

"Because that's the way God made the world."

"So, do God got Gina?"

"Yes. she is with God."

"Can you take me to God so I can see Gina?"

"I wish it was that easy, Miracle. No, I can't take you to God."

"Why?"

"Because he is not here."

"Well where's he at dad?"

"He lives in heaven and heaven is up in the sky."

"So nobody can take you there. So, how did Gina get to God's house?

"God came and got her when she died."

"Dad, who is God really?"

Right then, Keith knew he was wrong for keeping Miracle out of church. Gina used to take her to church all the time. And now she was asking him questions he really did not know.

"Miracle God is our father."

"I thought you were my father."

"I am your father, but God is all of our father."

"So, I got two fathers?"

"Yeah, everybody got two fathers."

"If he my father, then why I can't go to his house or talk to him?"

"You can talk to him any time. But you just can't see him."

"That's crazy, daddy. How can I talk to him if I can't see him?"

Keith thought about how she liked to pray.

"Okay you know how you say grace before you eat and how you pray before you go to sleep. When you do that, you are talking to God."

"Well dad, I never hear God talk back. I always do all the talking. So next time I pray, I will ask about Gina."

"You can ask God anything baby he will listen. I've got to start taking you to church, and when you get in the church, ask those people all the questions you want about God. They will tell you. Plus, I want to hear what they say. But right now, let's finish this work so we can go have fun."

Keith had to get his job schedule to work around Miracle's hours. Being that he had been working there for a while and the loss of his wife, his boss had no problem with helping out with his hours. He dropped most of his late hours so he could pick Miracle up from school.

She caught the school bus in the morning. Miracle was not friendly at all. She was very antisocial. When she got on the bus, she would only speak to the bus driver, and this morning it was no difference.

"Hello Mr. Tony," she said and sat right behind Tony, the bus driver. The only thing she liked about school was her work. She didn't even like her teacher.

"There go the nerd girl y'all!" A skinny tall black boy yelled from the back of the bus and pointed at Miracle. All the other kids on the bus burst out laughing. Miracle hated the fact that she always gets picked on. She just kept quiet and never said anything back. She knew they would leave her alone in a little bit.

The bus driver always looked at her strange. Tony tried to figure out who this little girl looked like to him. He knew she looked very familiar; he just could not put his finger on it. He dealt with so many kids and the kids' parents that he could not remember. He didn't know any Marshalls and her last name was Marshall. He just pushed the thought to the back of his head. He liked how polite the little girl was and respectful. She always spoke to him and carried herself as a young woman. Tony pulled up to the school bus ramp and all the kids got off. He drove the bus for the school levels, from elementary school to junior high school to high school. He liked his job driving around all day. He was always ready to work. The money was needed providing for two kids. Plus, driving kids around was not hard at all. He dropped the kids off then drove to his next route.

Miracle was seven years old and placed up to the fourth grade. That was very charming to her teacher. She never needed any help with her work, and she was so neat. The youngest and already the head of her class. Being brown skinned and short with mid weight made her look even cuter. She had thick eyebrows and long straight black hair. The subject that she liked the most was Reading. Gina always used to read to her, and Gina would listen to her read. When she read, she thought about Gina so much. That made her miss Gina even more. She just could not understand why God took Gina if God was so nice like people say he is. The only friend she had now was Keith, her daddy, and she loved him so much. He was so nice and always so caring to her. She just hoped that God would not take her dad like he did her mom. Because then, she would not have no one and she would not know what to do.

"Mrs. Moody, I'm done with my work," Miracle said to her teacher.

"Okay Miracle, just read a book until everyone else gets done and then we will all go over it together and make sure everyone understands."

"Yes ma'am," Miracle said, then pulled out her History book to read.

Some of the other kids looked at her and could not believe that she was done already. They knew she was smart when their teacher told them that she is a second grader that works on fourth grade level. Some of the kids wished that they were smart like her and some of them could not stand her. They felt so jealous of her. Plus, with her always wearing nice clothes and new shoes, most of them did not like her and they wanted her to go to another class. But their teacher was so happy to have Miracle in their class. She liked it so much that she even talked about Miracle to her husband at home. A lot of the teachers in that school came by her classroom just to meet Miracle. They all knew of her daddy, the great professor at the college UCF. Now, they see all his smarts paying off. At the school meeting two weeks ago, they were talking about putting Miracle in the school Spelling Bee. She was a very gifted little girl and a very fast learner. You had no choice but to be proud of her. Every day she did her best just like she was told to do. She was so much more mature than the other kids because she only spent time with adults. She never played with other kids. All she did was study and study more.

Chapter 10

Time seemed to be going by fast. Miracle was now ten and she had a new friend named Tiffany, who taught her so much about God. That is what made Miracle happy to go to church. Now she understood a lot about God. Keith knew now that church was needed. No matter what you are going through in life, turn to God and give God your problems. Now he was stronger, wiser, and feeling better. Keith and Miracle went to church together with Tiffany and they always had a good time. Tiffany was really a God fearing woman that loved to go to church. If a person did not know any better, you would think that Tiffany and Keith were a couple. But they were so far from being a loving couple. They were great friends that needed someone to talk to from time to time. Tiffany enjoyed the good feeling of bringing people closer to God. She knew God was using her as he pleased.

She always prayed for her lil baby girl. That was something that she could not push out her mind. She was to the point in her life that she was willing to give motherhood another try. Being around Miracle made her think of being a mother so much. But she just was not blessed with the right guy yet. In due time, she knew God would bless her to be happy. She ate healthy and she worked out to keep her health up. On passing routes, she saw Tony, but they never spoke to each other. They locked eyes a few times and the love and care she felt for him was still there. She still wished that they could be together now. It'd been a little over ten years since a man has touched her. The need for sex died down once she got into God.

Keith was a nice guy, and she gave him so much respect for being a wonderful father. He did all he could for his lil girl. He spoiled her to death. But the main thing he did with her was spend time with her. He taught her everything. They studied at least twice a day. It was so cute how that little girl wanted to be a surgeon. She gave her all to learn she would not give up no matter how hard the work got. She practiced on dummy dolls that Keith brought her. He even timed her and stopped the test when she did wrong, letting her know that she just lost a patient. She tried harder on the next test. She practiced on all types of surgeries. From brain to heart to kidneys. The need to help people was really in her. From the loss of Gina, her goal was to save lives. When she prayed, she promised Gina that she would be the best surgeon ever.

Chapter 11

"**D**addy, daddy, help me please!" Miracle yelled out at 2:17 in the morning from her bedroom.

Keith jumped out of his bed still sleep and slipped and fell over his cover that was wrapped around his feet. His heart raced and his mind was in panic mode from hearing Miracle scream out like that. She had just turned twelve five months ago, and everything was going so good for them.

"Help me daddy, please!"

Keith jumped up off the floor and ran as fast as he could to Miracle's room. He turned on her room light and she was sitting up in her bed crying with blood all over her covers. She looked up at him with tears running down her face and asked him, "Daddy, what is wrong with me?"

Keith knew exactly what was going on. Miracle had just got her period. Something he never told her about. All he could do was stand there and stare at her until his thoughts caught up with him. He did not know what to do. He was never prepared for this.

"Miracle, it is okay," he said as he walked up to her.

"It's blood everywhere," she said as she cried.

"I know baby but it's okay."

He knew how terrified Miracle was of blood. Plus, he did not have a clue on how to explain this to her.

"Why am I bleeding like this dad? I don't want to die," Miracle said then jumped up out of her bed and ran to the bathroom.

Keith followed behind her trying to figure out how he could talk to her about this. When he got to the bathroom, Miracle was sitting up in the tub with all her clothes on. It was clear to see through her silk nightgown that blood was still rushing from in between her legs. Keith turned the cold water on and sat down on the toilet lid next to the tub so he could talk to her.

"Miracle, stop crying and listen to me please."

She looked up at him with so much concern in her pretty eyes. "What is wrong with me?"

"Nothing is wrong with you. By you being a young woman now, this is something that is going to happen to you every month."

"What? Why?" Miracle yelled out.

"I really do not know. All I do know is that it is something that happens to all females. It's not bad and no you are not going to die. But you will bleed like this once a month around the same time. It's called a cycle or a period."

"I don't want to bleed like this. How can I stop it?"

Now for the first time pads and tampons popped into his mind. He remembered throwing the ones Gina had away. So, he knew that it was none in the house.

"Miracle, you will be bleeding for about seven days. I got to go to the store and get you something for the pain, blood and to keep you clean. So while I'm gone, clean yourself up and calm down. Miracle, don't you know by being a surgeon that you are going to see a lot of blood?"

"Yes I know that. But as long as it is not my blood, I don't care. Now you can go. Hurry up and come back."

Keith went to the store with so much on his mind. He bought a bottle of Midol pills and a bottle of Advil pills. He also bought some pads and tampons. While he was looking he got a bottle of Vagisil. When he got to the cashier, she was a young Spanish girl about twenty one years old. The look that she gave him when he placed his items on the counter made him realize what he was really buying. Keith wanted to ask her for some help with his problem, but he bit his tongue and just went off his own concept. He just got some of the things he saw Gina with. Keith thought to himself on why in the hell they did not adopt a boy? Because raising a girl was really hard for a man. Keith loved Miracle to death, but still it was a lot of shit he wished he did not have to see or do. What he was going through was the main one.

"Seventeen dollars and thirty three cents, sir," the young cashier said to Keith once she rung and bagged everything up. Keith paid her and left thinking about Miracle and what the hell was he about to do. A lot of things that he was supposed to be telling her he forgot.

"Lord please give me the wisdom and strength to raise and help this little girl," Keith prayed out loud as he drove home.

Miracle was laying in the tub sideways all balled up from cramping. Keith walked into the bathroom and just looked at her for a couple seconds. When she saw Keith, she tried to smile but he knew it was a fake smile.

"Are you okay?" Keith asked her.

"No, my stomach is hurting so bad.

"I got some pills for you. It should help with the pain. I'm going to go downstairs and get you a glass of water."

"No!" She screamed out. "Just give me the damn pills," she said with so much anger in her voice.

Keith never heard her speak like that. It took him by surprise. He didn't know if he was wrong or not. He handed her both bottles of pills. She took two of each without any water.

"I got you some more stuff, but you have to figure out which one or should I say what kind you want to use." He took the tampons out of the bag and held them up for her to see. "If you use this kind to stop the bleeding, you will have to stick it up inside of you. If you do not like that, then you can use this kind," he said and held the pads. "You can place one of these in the crotch of your panties and it will stop the blood from getting all over the place. Both of these products will stop blood from getting everywhere. So once you get all cleaned up, choose one."

While Keith talked, Miracle noticed that the pain stopped, and the blood flow slowed down until almost a stop. Keith took everything out of the bag and sat them on the toilet lid.

51

"What is that water for?" Miracle asked and pointed at the douche bottle.

"Oh um it's not water. Once your cycle is complete in seven days, you have to stick this tip inside of you and squeeze real hard and fast until it's empty. So it will clean you out and get rid of the smell."

For the first time, Miracle looked up at Keith like "What." Keith smiled and walked out of the bathroom and closed the door behind him. Then, he took a real deep breath...

***

Miracle told Tiffany what had happened to her five days ago while they were in church. Tiffany laughed at Miracle and explained everything to her about having a cycle. Then, she looked over at Keith and smiled a big smile. Just picturing him acting the way Miracle said he did. *Poor Keith* is what went through her mind. They enjoyed their day at church together. Being around Miracle made Tiffany feel good in an odd way. Once church was over and everyone was leaving, Keith sat in the car waiting on Miracle to finish saying her goodbyes. He watched as she hugged Tiffany and swore to himself that they looked just alike. Miracle looked like a little Tiffany. Maybe because they spent so much time together or maybe because he got used to seeing them all the time. Miracle got into the car, and they drove home.

"Are you ready for your test today?" He asked her.

"Yes, I'm ready. I been thinking about it all day."

"It's really hard but I still want you to go through with it. Because in order to be the best, you have to pass all the hard tests twice. So relax and take your mind off anything that is worrying you. You are still young, and you have so much more to learn."

Miracle's mind was still on the fact that Tiffany just told her that she was moving away in two days. She was moving out of state so she could get better care for her condition. Tiffany was the only friend Miracle had so it really did hurt her that Tiffany was moving away. Once they got home, Keith prepared the test for her. Even though she did not feel like taking the test, she did anyway, and she did her best. She did not want Keith to feel as if he was wasting his time. So she got over the thought of Tiffany. One thing that she knew was that in life you gain and in life you lose. So, she kept to her way of living.

Chapter 12

Betty, who got locked up the same night she dropped Miracle off at 7-Eleven, was finally free. After serving twelve long years for robbery, she was so happy to be out. She made an oath to better herself and to get a job. She walked all the way to the unemployment office on her first day out. She filled out the forms for all the fast food help wanted ads. Once she got done there, she went and checked into a shelter. She never wanted to stay behind a dumpster again. She felt that bad luck struck her once she left that little baby at that store. She could not forget that night for some reason. She also wondered how things turned out for that little baby. She was so happy that she did not get a charge for that baby. When she got to the shelter, it was time for dinner. After she ate, she showered up, got into her bed and read her bible. Then, she prayed before she went to sleep…

***

"Hello, Mr. Marshall. My name is Sophy Jones, " a high yellow thick curvy female said to Keith sticking out her hand.

Keith looked up from his desk then stood up to greet her.

"Hello Ms. Jones," Keith said as he shook her hand. "How may I help you?"

"I'm a new teacher here and I have heard so many great things about you. I decided to come meet you for myself."

"Well that's very nice of you Ms. Jones. I hope you enjoy your stay here."

"Thank you," she said and turned to walk away.

Then, she turned back toward Keith and said, "How about dinner tonight?"

It took Keith by total surprise. He had not been with a woman since Gina. So out of loneliness he said, "Yes, at my place."

Plus, Sophy was a very attractive female. They switched numbers and she left. Keith felt good and bad at the same time. But he knew that he needed some happiness in his life. Plus, it was odd that he could not stop thinking of Sophy. For the rest of his day at work, he kept picturing how pretty and curvy Sophy was.

Once he picked Miracle up from school, he told her about Sophy coming over for dinner. He also wanted to know how she felt about it. She smiled and said, "I think it's nice for you daddy. I'll help cook dinner. I think that we should make stuffed bell peppers and crab cakes. Dad, I want you to be happy and I feel that you need a friend. I don't feel no funny type of way about that. I also can't wait to meet her. I just hope she is cool."

Keith was happy that Miracle really understood life.

"Thank you," he said and patted her on the head.

"Just promise me daddy that you will never let no one come between us."

"I promise."

"No! Look me in my eyes and tell me."

Keith looked at Miracle's serious face and swore he was looking at Tiffany. He looked into Miracle eyes and said I promise.

"Have you heard from Mrs. Tiffany, Miracle?"

"No," she said sadly and stared out the passenger side window.

He noticed that was a soft spot for her. The more he looked at her, the more she looked like Tiffany. Keith just shook his head and drove home. He could not understand why this little girl looked so much like Tiffany to him. Then, he thought maybe he was missing Tiffany. Did he like her? She was a beautiful female. He didn't know. But he did know that this was the second time Miracle looked like Tiffany to him. Once they got home, Miracle asked.

"What time is she coming?"

Keith looked at his watch and said, "She will be here in two hours."

"Well dad, you go ahead and take a shower. I'll wash my hands and start the food. Then, once you get ready, you can finish the food while I get ready."

"Sounds like a deal to me," Keith said and went upstairs.

Miracle went to the kitchen and went to work. By the time Keith came back downstairs looking all handsome and smelling good, the food was completely done. It was fifteen minutes until Sophy was supposed to be there. Keith looked at the food and smiled. He told Miracle thanks on her way upstairs. Soon as she reached the top, the doorbell rang. Miracle noted that Mrs. Sophy was the type of person that likes to be early. Keith opened the door, and he was shocked. Sophy looked so stunning. In her pink tight MK dress and shoes, her hair was pinned up and she smelt wonderful. She smiled while Keith just stared at her curvaceous figure.

"Well, may I come in," she said to break the odd moment.

"Oh yes. Excuse my manners. Hello and come in."

She walked in and looked around. She liked what she saw but the pictures of Gina and Miracle.

"Have a seat," Keith said and turned on the TV.

As Sophy sat down, he looked at her again to make sure he saw what he really saw. And it was true, her dress was see through. He could see nothing but cocoa brown nipples. She did not have a bra on and her little pink panties barely covered anything. He sat next to her, and she moved closer to him.

"So, what do you like to watch?"

"I'm here for you, Keith. Whatever you wish, I will follow."

She was so close that her breath tingled his neck. And his dick started to swell.

"So, how long have you been staying here?"

"About fifteen years now."

"I got to tell you that this is a nice place."

"Thank you."

She didn't dare to ask about the two females she seen on the pictures, because she didn't care for them at all. As long as he didn't bring them up, she would act like she never saw them.

"Keith, you are a very good looking man. So, what made you want to teach?"

"I guess because I enjoy learning and teaching people makes me feel good."

"Well, I need you to teach me a couple of things and I'm not talking about schoolwork."

She was trying not to come on too strong but this man was who and what she wanted. He was so attractive and he got money. So if she had to sleep with him, she was ready. Keith felt so shy and boyish around her, and he didn't know why. It has been so long that he had a female attention this way. He did not want to tell her to stop.

"Tell me something about you, Sophy. Are you new in town?"

"Yes, I got referred to UCF, so I took the job. And look what I found," she said and rubbed the back of his ear lightly.

She saw his dick jump to her soft touch and she rubbed his ear again. She knew right then that she had him.

"So," she got closer so that her nipples could rub against him.

"Hello, how are you?" Miracle said, stepping off the last step.

Neither one of them saw her until she spoke.

"Who the hell is she?" Sophy asked bitterly.

"I'm Miracle," she said and dropped the smile from her face.

"Sophy, that's my daughter, Miracle. And Miracle, this is Sophy."

"Your daughter? You didn't tell me you had kids."

Miracle sensed the dislike from Sophy.

"I didn't have to tell you. As long as you know now. That is what matters."

Keith did not like the way Sophy acted towards Miracle. Sophy was steaming inside.

"Dad, are you and Mrs. Sophy ready to eat?"

"Yes, we are."

"So tell me, where is her mother Keith?"

"Sorry to say that she passed a while back."

Now that brightened Sophy's mood a little bit.

"Oh, I'm so sorry to hear that. I apologize to you and Miracle."

Sophy and Keith got up to meet Miracle in the kitchen.

"It smells good in here. What are we eating?"

Miracle was so happy to cook for people. We are having crab and shrimp stuffed bell pepper and crab cakes.

"Wow, who cooked this meal?"

"I did," Miracle said smiling.

"You?"

"Yes ma'am."

"Please call me Sophy. I want us to get along very good. And if you don't mind, can I help you fix our plates?"

"Yes please, that will be great."

Miracle looked at Sophy's outfit and wondered why she was dressed that way. Sophy was very pretty and had a nice body. Miracle couldn't understand why she was dressed so nasty. Then, she thought maybe this is how you dress when you go meet a guy. Maybe she could learn a lot from Sophy. She hoped that Keith would like Sophy so she could get a chance to learn some things from her. At first, Sophy seemed mean to her but now she seemed cool. They all ate. Keith and Sophy told Miracle how great the food was. Thank you and thank you is all she could say. She felt so special and grown. Miracle gathered up all their plates and put them in the dishwasher.

"How old are you, Miracle?" Sophy asked.

"I'm twelve and a half."

"So what you're ... in the sixth grade right?"

"No ma'am, I'm in the ninth grade."

"You're in the ninth grade at the age of twelve?" Sophy asked with excitement in her voice.

"Yes, I skipped two grades because those classes were too slow."

Now that's so nice to hear, Miracle. I think it is a blessing from God for people to be smart like that.

"Yes I agree but you got to give my dad thanks too. He is my teacher in all that I do."

Sophy looked at Keith who was smiling brightly. Then, thought about the mama that she seen on the picture. And thought that this lil girl do not look like either one of them.

"You taught her on a college level, Keith?"

"Yes and we still got a lot of studying to do."

"So do you guys want butter pecan ice cream for dessert?"

"Sure," Sophy said, stuck in a little trance.

She was thinking that this man really has his shit together. And if she was going to have a shot to get him, she would have to get pregnant from him to take the attention off this lil spoiled brat. Because this little girl was too damn much at the age of twelve. She carried herself as if she was about seventeen. Plus, she was very smart and held a strong impact on Keith.

"One scoop or two scoops, Ms. Sophy?"

"Um two please," she said and smiled a fake smile at Miracle.

"Sophy, what subject are you teaching?" Keith asked.

"American History. Something that everyone thinks is so boring."

Miracle burst out laughing so hard that Keith joined in laughter with her. Miracle handed both of them their ice cream cones. Then went to fix hers. Sophy licked and sucked on her ice cream cone so seductively while looking Keith in his eyes. She made sure she did it while Miracle had her back turned. Keith stared back at her not out of horniness but out of dislike. Her style as a woman was way below his radar. *How can a female this pretty be so trashy?* He felt she had all the signs of a whore.

"Do you have any kids?" He asked.

"No, I have not been blessed in that aspect. Also, I only tried three times. Men these days are not what they seem to be."

"Oh really. Miracle, can you leave me and Mrs. Sophy alone for a while?"

"Yes sir," she said and took her ice cream to her room.

"It's about time you did that," Sophy said.

"Listen Sophy, what's your problem?"

"What do you mean, Keith?

"First of all, you come to my house dressed like a stripper and on top of that, you're acting like a one night whore. And the main thing you have showed nothing but disrespect to my daughter. So, tell me, what the hell are you trying to prove?

"Honestly Keith, I come from a hard life. I have been on my own since my stepfather paid my mom to have sex with me. My mom was strung out on heroin, so she didn't care. I was only fourteen when my stepfather walked in on me taking a shower. I was so scared, and I was in shock. I screamed for my mom. He told me don't yell for her because she has been paid for this. I was completely naked, and he raped me. I tried my best to fight back. But he was too strong and fighting back only made it hurt more. After that, I ran away. I started stripping at a very young age to make it. I was not into selling my body. But no matter how hard it was for me, I still stayed in school. And it finally paid off. So to get what I want, I give it my all. Now if you feel I'm coming on too strong, it's just me. I get straight to the point. I mean what's the big secret. If we like each other, we gone end up fucking anyway. So, why wait? Now I dress like this because I don't like to be turned down. Now the deal with Miracle is, I did not know you had kids. So I was very upset about the way that I found out. Plus if you had told me you had a kid in the house I would have not dressed this way. I'm human, Keith. I got feelings."

"I understand all that, Sophy. But let me walk you to your car."

"Are you serious, Keith?"

"Yes!"

So it's like that?"

"I just think it's time for you to go and I did enjoy your company. Thank you for coming."

"Bye Keith," she said and left.

Chapter 13

Tiffany enjoyed herself in Boston. She found a nice church and joined it. She even preached on and off at times. She had her own place, and she was still single. She had a job in a Super Walmart in the service department. She was really good when it came to dealing with people. She always thought of how her life would be if she had kept her child. Would it have been a setback? She really hated the fact that she got rid of her lil baby girl. But she felt like that is what changed her and got her right with God.

Living up north was way harder than living down south. She had to get used to the bus routes and work her work schedule around the bus time. That was her way of transportation because she hated to drive in the snow. She kept her car parked in the winter. Not too often but at times, she thought about Keith and Miracle. She had nothing but good memories of them two. Specially Keith, he was so handsome with a nice body. The perfect man for any female would be Keith. She admired the way he took care of his little girl. He made sure that he spent a lot of time with her and brightened her up on all levels. She could see herself with Keith but being that he lost his wife, she just showed sorrow. Still to this day, she felt good about getting them two back into church and trusting in God. One day she planned on going back and paying them a visit. She watched lil Miracle grow up and learn so much. She missed them deeply, but she just didn't want to admit it. Living by herself, she was so lonely. But let the truth be told, she was so happy. For the last couple of days, she had meant to call Miracle, but she fought against it. She did not want to be a part of Miracle life if she could not be there. She prayed for them every day and kept to her busy life. Boston provided better care for her condition with good cheap specialists to monitor her. Even the medication was better along with the health assistant. So the cold weather was something she just has to get used to.

***

Saturday morning, Sophy sat on her bed watching cartoons. It has been three months since her and Keith had their little fallout but at work he always spoke to her. He never ate lunch with her. She was still trying to figure him out. She felt that her feelings was the reason they didn't just kick things off. She always moved fast because slow people miss out on so much in life. The only thing she wanted was a family. The last time she had been with a man was two years ago. He was a street thug that sold drugs and went to jail often. She lost feelings for him once she found out everything about him. They were together for ten months and she only fucked him twice. Then, she told him that she had a change of heart. Now, she was to the point of being tired of being lonely. She was light skinned with a very nice curvy body. She was very smart, and had no kids. The qualities she had she wanted the same in her man.

Having nothing but a bra and panties on, she got up and went to look at herself in her full length mirror. She was so happy with her shape. She worked out hard to keep her figure. As she looked into the mirror, she pushed her tits up and made a sexy face. Then, she gripped her nice fat butt and blew a kiss at herself in the mirror. She smiled because she knew she was sexy. *Why can't you get a good man?* She asked herself out loud still looking into the mirror.

She kept her pussy hair shaved very low, almost bald. She stared at how fat her pussy print looked in her panties. She placed her right hand on top of her panties and held her pussy in her hand. Then, she started to rub back and forth slowly. She moaned lightly when she felt the dampness in her panties from her wet pussy. She took off her bra and her nipples were rock hard. She grabbed one of her 36 DDs, licked the nipple then sucked on it.

She walked inside her room bathroom and got her two dildos out of the cabinet. She slid her panties off on the bathroom floor and dropped down on her knees. She stuck one of the ten inch dildos in her mouth while she squeezed and rubbed the other one. Then, she bent over the tub in a doggystyle position while she sucked and spit on the dildo in her mouth with her eyes closed. Her pretty pussy was getting wetter and wetter. She could feel her juices sliding down her thighs. She took the dildo out her mouth and arched her back. She spread her legs open wider and slid it slowly inside her wet warm pussy. As she pushed it all the way inside her, she moaned out loud. Then, she placed the other dry dildo in her mouth. She was on her knees doggystyle, bent over the tub pushing one dildo in and out her mouth and another one in and out of her pussy. She sucked and pushed harder.

As she pushed the dildo in and out of her, she felt herself about to climax. Instead of pushing in her, she started jamming it inside of her. She felt her little pussy tighten up as she came all on the dildo. She slid it in and out of her real slow to spit her cum all over it. Once she finished cumming on it, she slid it out of her pussy and licked it. She started sucking on it and swallowing her own cum. She turned over and laid with her back flat on the floor. She never took the dildo out her mouth. Her cum tasted too good. She opened her legs up as wide as she could and slid the other dildo up and down her pussy slit like a credit card. She stuck it in her overly wet pussy. She speeded the pace up to match her mood. She came so fast that way that she was upset. She came on the dildo. She took it in and out of her to rub her slippery cum on the tip of her asshole. She pushed the dildo slowly and carefully into her asshole. Once she got it half way in her ass, she took the other dildo out her mouth and slid it inside her pussy. She pushed both dildos all the way in her at the same time and felt both of her holes throbbing.

"Shit!" She screamed out loud and for the first time, she opened her eyes. But it felt too good for her to stop. She put one of her titty nipples in her mouth and sucked on it to keep from screaming out loud. She worked both of her holes until she orgasmed and started shaking. She spit her titty nipple out of her mouth before she pulled the dildo out of her ass and sucked on it while she finished cumming on the other one.

In her mind, she felt like how could you ask a guy to eat your ass if you would not do it or at least taste it? She sucked the dildo clean then pulled the one out her pussy and sucked on it as she got up off the floor and walked back into her bedroom. She went and picked out her best porn flick online. She still had the dildo in her mouth when the porn flick started. Now, she was hot and ready to fuck. She could copy every move on the porn flick since she just warmed herself up.

Miracle had the surgeon tactic down all the way over. All the years of studies that her and Keith did really made her out to be great. She was so hyped on how she passed all the tests twice that Keith gave her. He even did a pop quiz on her that she flew through. She was ready to move on to the next level. She knew how to place all patients under medication to stable their condition to start surgery. She knew how to remove all organs but she did not know how to replace them. What she did not know was the hardest part. But a good thing about her was that she did not forget nothing, and she loved to learn. She read and she practiced three times a day. She really wanted this more than anything else in her life.

She never went outside to play or had any friends. She have been grown since she was born.

She did not know what being a kid was. All she knew was to start and finish anything she wanted. Even though Keith took her to the movies and to theme parks, that did not amaze her. She wanted knowledge at all times. If she liked you then that meant she could learn from you. She didn't want baby dolls and toys. She wanted books and tests. If she failed or could not do something right, she would get so mad at herself and would not sleep for a while from studying so much. The biggest task for her was to fail. Keith taught her that no one was better than her in anything and that she could do anything she put her mind to do. That stuck with her. She never wanted to fail. It made her feel like she was letting Keith down. She did not want Keith to feel like he was wasting his time. So to be the best, she gave it her best and did her best. Tomorrow will be her first lesson on how to place organs back into the body.

The next morning, Keith surprised her with Dr. Wheelin. He was the best surgeon on the east coast. He was the number one surgeon and what made him the best was the fact that he never lost a patient. That is also why he was so expensive. Most families picked him to perform on their loved ones. But the price to get him was the matter for most low income families. Dr. Wheelin was also a chief professor at UCF, so Keith has gotten the chance to become real close to him over the years. Keith had told him all about Miracle years ago. And now he had to let Dr. Wheelin know that all the lessons that he's been giving to him, Miracle had mastered. Dr. Wheelin could not believe that a little twelve year old could be that smart. He had to come and see for his self. Now if it turned out that she was so gifted, he would love to work with her personally. Miracle knew exactly who he was. She have read so many of his books and watched more than enough of his videos. She was so overjoyed to meet him in person.

"Hello, Dr. Wheelin, how are you this morning?" She asked.

"I'm good and I'm so grateful to be here to see how much you have learned. From my understanding, your father tells me that you are well more advanced than the lessons I sent."

"Yes sir, I have been studying real hard since I was seven."

Dr. Wheelin and Keith both laughed at her seriousness.

"Well, I'm gone leave you two alone," Keith said. "And if you two need anything, I'll be in my office."

"Okay, little genius, let's get started because you know time is money. Specially in the profession you've taken up."

Miracle just smiled and watched his every move. She wanted to be great just like him or better.

"Dr. Wheelin, when I become a surgeon do I get to tell the people how much money I want for helping them?"

"Why yes," Dr. Wheelin said.

"Then that's good because I'm gone to do it for free."

"Are you crazy little girl? How will you pay your bills?"

"I don't know yet, but I do know that I want to help people."

"Miracle listen, helping people comes with the job, and charging people comes with the job. People pay you to save lives. Plus, you will have to keep your policy covered. It's okay to have a good heart and to care for people. But you have to realize that it costs to live. Now that's enough about that, let's get started."

Dr. Wheelin placed one of his test dummies on the table. The clothes on the dummy were ripped and the dummy had blood all over it. He told Miracle that the dummy had just been shot and is suffering from a punctured lung and heart failure. That his condition is very poor, and time is running out. He must be saved now.

" So I want you to perform what you know. I'm starting the time, now."

Miracle eyes were wide open with fear. Once she saw all that blood, it freaked her out. Even though the blood was not real, it still shook her up. The dummies that Keith tested her with never had blood on them. Much as she hated blood, she still placed on her gloves and did her best. She used Dr. Wheelin as her nurse assistant. Once she got the dummy stable and on medication, she cut it open. She jumped when she saw the heart beating. That was new to her. But she knew by studying that if the heart still beats, then it's still good. She looked at his organs very carefully and quickly.

"Dr., nothing inside of him needs to be moved. I'll pinch his lung back to close the wound. Also, his heart still has a beat. It's poor but it's enough for you to install a pacemaker."

"Miracle, I'm not the surgeon you are."

"But I don't know how to install anything yet," she said so sadly.

"Well then, I guess your patient will die."

Miracle thought real hard on what to do. She felt that she could not fix his lung with a poor heartbeat. That she had to put the pacemaker in first. With so much running through her mind while Dr. Wheelin watched, she did all she could and tried to remember all that she studied. Once she felt that everything was complete, she stepped back and let Dr. Wheelin go over her work while she bit down on her bottom lip. It didn't even take him two minutes to tell her that she just lost a patient. She felt so lost and out of place. Her mind went blank, and she cried until he told her that it is okay because she had no idea on what to do. So once he starts showing her through studying that she will understand a lot better and easier because she will be very familiar with the organs.

Chapter 14

Sophy kept herself respected in the school. She carried herself very professionally in front of others. You would never think that she came from a rough childhood. She was very proud of herself no matter what other people thought of her. The only thing that she longed for was a good man. She didn't want just to embrace anyone. She wanted Keith in her life. Someone she could grow with. They both continued to eat lunch together every day. Then, they got to the point that they really started talking. As Keith spent time with her, he learned more about her. He was now understanding why she was the way she is. She really had trust issues and a lack of confidence. But she was very clean and intelligent. Today while they ate lunch together, she asked Keith.

"So, what were your wife's name?"

"Well that is strange that you asked. It's like I have not talked about her since she passed."

"Well, don't you think it's about time that you stop holding all that in and let it out. Trust me, Keith, it will make you feel a lot better."

"I guess you are right. Her name was Gina."

"That's a very nice name."

So tell me more about her. Sophy knew how to play her cards. She knew she had to get Keith to open up to her about his wife so he could start to feel lonely for a woman. She had to soften him up and make him feel somewhat comfortable with her. He could find it very easy to lean on her.

"Sophy, it's so much to tell you about her that I really don't know where to start. I can tell you this that Gina was very beautiful, inside and out, and she was a very hard worker."

"What type of work did she do?"

"She was the top real estate agent for celebrities."

"Wow! That's great."

"Now I see why you all daughter is so smart."

"Yeah, Gina loved Miracle very much, and Miracle loved her the same. Actually, I think that Miracle is just now getting over the hurt and the fact that Gina is gone. That's why Miracle is studying to be a surgeon. So she can save lives and stop people from dying," Keith said with a smile on his face thinking about Miracle.

"How old was Miracle when Gina died?"

"I think she was four. Now that was one of the hardest things I ever had to do was telling that lil girl that her mama was dead."

While Keith talked, a tear dropped out of his right eye. Sophy knew that he was very touched by the subject.

"I'm sorry, Keith. We can change the subject."

"Yes, I think that will be best," Keith said.

Sophy stood up and wiped the tear from Keith's face.

"Thank you," he said.

"You are welcome. So, when are you going to come visit me at my place? Let me cook for you and we both have a nice cup of wine."

"I think I just might take you up on that offer. So, when do you want to plan this nice meal for me?"

Sophy thought before she answered.

Then said, "Tomorrow at five. That's not too soon for you, is it?"

"No, I'll explain things to Miracle, and I'll be there."

"Well Keith, I don't want Miracle to feel completely left out. So, tell her that we will spend the weekend together. That way I can repay her for that nice meal she fixed for me."

"I will tell her, but she has been so busy studying with Dr. Wheelin that I don't know if she will go or not."

"That lil girl need a break from all that studying, Keith."

"Yeah I agree with you but that is how she been all her life. She is only interested in learning."

"Well, I think she is old enough to learn how to be a woman and I'm going to teach her if she lets me. That way she will know how to enjoy life instead of being stuck in the house all the time."

"Sophy please, do understand that Miracle is not like most kids. She don't care for friends or gifts. She only wants books and more books. So don't think that she are being funny if she says no or don't cling to you. She are very respectful to everyone. But she has never been friendly. But I sure will talk to her about spending some girl time with you so she can enjoy herself. Now listen Sophy, I love Miracle with all my heart. Don't ever let anything happen to her or teach her anything wrong. I will never forgive you if you do."

"Keith, listen, even though I don't have any kids, that don't mean I don't know how to be a mother, and a great one at that. I will never disrespect that little girl in any type of way. I know how it is to be raised the hard way and not loved. I was not born with a silver spoon in my mouth like Miracle. But I'm still a successful woman."

"Stop right there, Sophy. Because your childhood could not even come close to Miracle's childhood. That little girl is not me and Gina's biological daughter. Gina could not have kids. She was not blessed in that department. So we decided to adopt a child so we could have a nice family. We picked Miracle out of the baby lineup. Babies who were not born with a silver spoon in her mouth at all. That adoption center named her Miracle because on the night that she was born, her parents abused her. They took her to a corner store and left her on the counter. She had a very bad bruise on the side of her head and left arm. So me and Gina both agreed to let her keep her name. Besides, it is a Miracle that that little girl lived. Now look at her. She has turned out to be a Miracle."

"Are you serious, Keith?"

"Yes!"

"Does she know that?"

"No, I don't know how to tell her yet. I'm going to wait until she gets older and have a very long talk with her."

"I would have never guessed that, Keith. They say it is always someone's life that is worse than yours. So that is why you love that little girl so much huh?"

"Yes I'm all that she has and plus, she makes me think of Gina so much. All Gina wanted was a baby and she was so happy about Miracle."

"One last question. How did Gina die?"

"She was in a very bad car accident that killed her on impact and the craziest thing about that is that it was on her birthday."

"What? Where is the mercy in this world? Shit talking about hard lives, Keith you had one."

Now that was the first time Keith thought of it that way. Everybody has a story to tell. After work, Keith explained everything to Miracle. She told him that she would not mind spending time with Sophy. As long as they planned things a day beforehand.

"Dad, can you please tell Ms. Sophy that she does not owe me anything for that dinner."

"I sure will let her know."

"So, do you really like her?" Miracle asked.

"Yeah I guess. She is kind of cool since I have got to know her a little better."

"I been seeing you smiling a little more dad so I can tell she makes you happy."

"You are right, Miracle. This side of me has been closed and shut down since Gina died, and I got to say that it do feel good to finally get back to being myself again. Well, since you are taking a break from studying, how about we go out and get some ice cream?"

"Dad, I'm not a little kid anymore."

"I know that, but I also know that you love butter pecan ice cream. Plus, the ride would be good for the both of us."

"Okay dad, you win. Let me save all my work and I'll be ready."

Keith watched her and thought how this girl is so much like Gina. Both of them studied so hard and never gave up. He remembered how Gina was still trying to study on the morning of their vacation.

"I'm ready, dad. All I have to do now is wash my hands."

They left and they both enjoyed themselves. While they were out, they even went out to dinner and rode around sightseeing and window shopping. By the time they got back home, they both were tired and sleepy. Miracle went to her room, showered up and went straight to sleep. Keith fixed him a strong drink and sat down on the edge of his bed thinking about Gina. He looked at the pictures of them together on his room dresser and did his silent crying as he did every other night while looking at their pictures. He finished his drink, said his prayers, showered up and went to sleep.

The next day seemed to move fast for Keith. When he looked at his watch, it was 3:33pm almost time for his date with Sophy. Miracle thanked him for picking her up from school. Something, she did every time. He did not know why she did, but he always just said no problem and you are welcome. He went upstairs, took a shower and got dressed. He told Miracle he was leaving and if she needed anything to make sure she called him.

When he rung Sophy's doorbell, it was 5:07pm. She opened the door and instead of saying hello, she said you are late. But then, she smiled and said come in, Keith. Soon as he walked in, he noticed that she had a thing for animals. She had a big bear skin rug on the floor, a stuffed tiger with its teeth showing. Plus, to top it all off, she had an oversized yellow, pink, and red parrot that sat in the corner of her living room. The bird kept saying hello how are you doing since Keith walked in. Her condo was very nice. She had style and great taste. The lights were turned down low and the soft music set the mood just right. The scented candles smelled so great. But the steak, potato and shrimp smelled even better. Sophy looked outstanding in her parish style Maxi dress.

She fixed them both a glass of wine. Then, she told Keith to please have a seat. They talked, laughed, and flirted with each other while they sipped their wine. Then, they went to the table and enjoyed their candle lit dinner. She fixed them both another glass of wine. They cuddled close to each other on the loveseat.

"Thank you Sophy, that meal was nice."

"Any time, Keith. I love to cook." He placed his arm around her neck and pulled her close to him. She smiled because it felt so good to her, and his body was so tight. She lifted his shirt up and started kiss on his stomach and licking on his navel. It felt so good to him that he just closed his eyes and let her do what she do. She undid his belt and his pants. He scooted down so she could try to get a better angle. She pulled out his manhood, kissed it, licked it and stuck it in her mouth. She did her best with her tongue ring, spit and lips. He came in her mouth, and she swallowed everything and kept sucking until his dick stood back up.

Once he got back rock hard, she pulled her dress up and straddled him. He pulled her dress all the way off and pushed her all the way down on his dick. She gasped from the pain and the great feeling of being penetrated. The feeling of warm wet pussy on his dick made Keith go wild. He started thrusting in and out of her so fast and hard that she came all over his dick. Not once but twice in eleven minutes. She could not control herself or figure out why she wanted to give herself completely to this man. He lifted her up off him and took all his clothes off. He laid her on the arm of the sofa with her back hanging halfway off and pushed her legs all the way back to her shoulders. Her little pussy was puffed out. He slid his dick inside her and held her steady so he could pound her like he wanted. He fucked her so roughly that she was in so much pain, but it felt so good at the same time. He speeded up when he felt himself about to cum. Sophy had tears running down the side of her face. It had been so long since Keith had some pussy that he did not realize just how hard and rough he was fucking her. He didn't even notice that she had gotten completely quiet. She felt like he was tearing her insides up. She closed her eyes tight and bit down on her bottom lip while she squeezed her couch pillows. She tried a couple times to push her legs down. But Keith held her too tight, and he was too strong. Plus, every time she tried to push her legs down, he pinned them up even higher. Keith felt himself cumming inside Sophy. He started to pull out but then thought against it and just let it flow all inside of her. Sophy was so happy and relieved when Keith was finished. Her pussy was sore and throbbing that she could feel it with a heartbeat.

"Damn girl, what you crying for?"

" Because it felt so good." She lied and smiled at him at the same time.

Keith sat down on the couch and took a couple deep breaths. Sophy got up and went to the bathroom to clean herself up. Then, she came out with a wet soapy rag and wiped Keith down. She tried to walk straight but she felt like she was knocked kneed, bowlegged and pigeon toed at the same time. Once they both got all cleaned up, she fixed them both another cup of wine. When Keith finished his drink, he got up and left.

Chapter 15

Tiffany was well advanced in her lifestyle up north. At first, it was hard but after six years things calmed down. She moved up to manager in the customer service department at Super Walmart. She still was not dating. She waited on the Lord to provide for her. She felt so good about herself and how far she had become. But at times, she felt so sick inside that she started working out and eating better two years ago. Her doctor still upgraded her medication and started monitoring her more and more. So, she knew that her condition was getting worse. Not only did she pray for better health, she also prayed for a donor. She tried her best to never let her sickness or pain show. She carried herself as the happiest person in the world. Church was great and always fulfilling to her soul. Her parents even came to visit her one week out of every year, and she finally told them that she had a baby and threw it in the dumpster. She described to them in full detail of the whole event. Her mom cried with her and held her at the same time.

"Baby in life you have to lose to gain, and may God forgive you for you know not what you did," is what her mom told her. Her dad just sat there quietly and let them have their moment. He was so surprised and mad, but he still loved his daughter wholeheartedly. They all prayed together that day in Tiffany's bedroom. And she promised that she would never keep a secret from them again.

Time went by so fast; six years just flew by. But each day that passed, she took a step forward. She has been doing her best every day that she kind of forgot about little Miracle. She was so busy in her life that thoughts about that little girl passed. Some nights, Tiffany cried herself to sleep by feeling sorry for herself. But most nights, she could not sleep at all by stressing about her health. All she wanted was a normal life with good health. Once that chapter was complete, she wanted a child that she could spoil and take care of but with a husband this time. Not no low life like Tony. She did not hate Tony. She just did not like his ways as a man. By him being older than her, she felt he could have at least told her that even if they are not together, they still would raise their child together. He made it seem like the baby is the reason that they fell out. So that is why she got rid of it. But the truth was that he did not want her anyway and Tony knew that. She knew that she would have kept her baby and not chase after Tony if he would have told her the truth. She blamed Tony for a lot because he knew. But she still blamed herself for being young and so stupid.

Miracle and Sophy chilled together more and more. To Miracle, Sophy could never be a mother figure, only a good friend. Miracle was eighteen and on her second year in college. She attended UCF and liked it. Plus, she wanted to be close to Keith and even more greater, Sophy was there. Miracle was so into her work that it all seemed easy to her. She have been studying since a kid and the college was behind on what she learned from

Keith and Dr. Wheelin. She got letters from many other schools trying to get her to pick their universities. Specially, the University of North Carolina at Chapel Hill. Even though they had better programs to offer her, she still stayed at UCF. Keith and Sophy were in a relationship. Sophy even moved into their house two years ago. Things seemed to be going very well and that was only when Sophy got her way. And most of the time she did because Miracle paid her no mind. Keith had a late meeting after school, so Sophy drove Miracle home.

"Miracle, how come you don't ask Keith to buy you a car?"

"Because he already knows that I don't like to drive."

"Why not?"

"Because that is how my mom, Gina died."

Sophy looked over at Miracle with a nasty look. She thought damn after all these years, she did not call me mom yet. But she is still calling this bitch, Gina mom.

"Miracle, how old are you?"

"I'm eighteen, why?"

"Because you are not a little girl anymore and it is about time that you woman up and know the truth."

"The truth about what?" Miracle asked as Sophy parked in the driveway.

Sophy faced Miracle.

"Now listen to me good, okay. Keith and Gina are not your real parents. You were adopted as a baby, and they raised you."

Miracle looked into Sophy's eyes to see if she was full of shit. Then she asked her, "What the hell are you talking about?"

"Are you listening to me, little girl? Smart as you are and now you are acting like you cannot comprehend simple things."

"No! Bitch! I comprehend very well. I just do not believe you and where did you get this lie from?"

"It's not a lie. It is the truth so do you understand that Keith and Gina are not your real parents."

"Well okay, Sophy since you know so much, who are my real parents? And please don't tell me you are."

"No! Of course I'm not and I have no idea who your real parents are."

"So, why are you telling me that I am adopted?"

"Because you are."

"Well, how do you know?"

"Because Keith told me a while back."

"You know what Sophy, you are a big liar, and I don't believe you. You can stop trying to become between me and my dad. And don't ever speak to me again. Besides, why in the hell will my dad tell you and not tell me if that is true?"

"I don't know all of that, Miracle but what I do know is Keith told me that."

"You are so evil Sophy," Miracle said and got out of Sophy's car.

She slammed the car door as hard as she could. She had so many thoughts in her head about

Sophy and all of them were bad. She could not wait to tell her dad what Sophy just said to her. She knew that Keith would kick Sophy out of their house for that stunt and that she wanted Sophy out tonight. She knew for a fact that Sophy was a liar, and she was not adopted. It was no way that Sophy was right. Keith would have told her a long time ago. Miracle stormed to her room with so much anger inside of her and locked her room door. She sat on her bed then pulled out her phone and called Keith. She called twice and both times it went to voicemail. Sophy knocked on Miracle's door. She felt so bad for Miracle. She didn't think that little girl would take it this hard. She thought that Miracle was just going to ask her a bunch of questions to get better understanding.

"Get away from my door. I do not want to talk to you."

"Well if you change your mind I'll be downstairs in the kitchen cooking. Don't forget that Keith will be gone for a while due to his late meeting."

Miracle laid back in her bed and covered up her head with her pillow. She wanted Sophy to leave her alone. Then, Miracle remembered the first night that she met Sophy at dinner. That night Sophy did ask Keith why she did not look like y'all. But Keith never answered, and Miracle never thought about asking him why he did not answer. Because she felt like he was just so happy and didn't hear Sophy clearly. She just needed to think and calm herself down. She could not fall for Sophy's trick. But she still could not figure out why Sophy would just lie to her like that. She fell asleep without even knowing it. She woke up out of her sleep not even knowing how long she been sleep. She called Keith's phone and he answered and told her to meet him downstairs. That he was about to walk into the house now. She jumped up out of bed and ran downstairs. Keith had just walked into the house and Sophy was walking up to him for a hug and kiss.

Miracle yelled out. "Dad don't touch her. She is a liar."

Sophy and Keith both looked at Miracle like she was crazy.

"Miracle, what is wrong with you?" Keith asked.

"She told me that I am adopted."

Sophy and Keith locked eyes.

"Why?" Keith said.

All Sophy could do was drop her head. Now Keith knew that he had to tell Miracle the truth. Even though he did not feel like it right now. He wanted it to be a much better moment than this.

Miracle smiled when she saw Sophy drop her head. And said, "Kick her out of our house for lying, dad. What, Sophy you must have thought I was not going to tell my dad that you lied."

"Miracle!" Keith raised his voice over hers. "Sophy did not lie. You are adopted."

Miracle felt as if she could not breathe. Her sight flashed before her, and she got very light headed. Even her hearing went out and her whole body felt numb.

"What! What did you just say dad?"

She knew damn well she did not hear him correctly. Tears ran down her face and her knee's got so weak that she fell down. Keith and Sophy both rushed over to her to pick her up. She pushed them both away from her as she got up off the ground.

"Tell me what did you say?" Miracle asked Keith again.

"I said yes that you are adopted. "I'm so sorry, Miracle. I know I should have told you a long time ago."

"Are you serious?" Miracle asked Keith and looked at him with hate in her eyes. "So you just gone let Sophy force you to lie to me?"

"Miracle, calm down and let me explain.

"No! I don't want you to explain shit to me. I don't even know who you really are. Dad or should I say Keith. Hell, I don't even know if that's your real name."

Miracle turned and walked back upstairs. She slammed her room door and started packing a small bag of her things. She pinched herself to see if she was dreaming. She got down on her knees and prayed. She cried and prayed until she had no more tears left. She got up, grabbed her small bag, and walked downstairs.

Sophy and Keith were talking. Keith jumped up when he saw her.

"Miracle, what is this?" He said and pointed at her bag.

"I'm leaving. I don't want to be here anymore."

"What? You can't just leave. Let's talk please."

"I have nothing to talk to you about. Since you talk to Sophy about everything, just keep talking to her," she said and walked out the front door.

Keith's heart dropped and he started going after Miracle. Sophy stopped him and told him that Miracle was just mad right now. Let her cool off for a little while. She will be back I promise. Give her a little while and then we will call her. If you chase her, it will only make her madder and she will really end up hating you.

"Yeah because of your big mouth!" Keith snapped on Sophy. "What put you in that position to say anything to her about that anyway? That was not your business to say anything to her about that. If it was not for you, this shit would not be happening."

"So what Keith, when was you gone tell the girl when she turns thirty? She is damn near twenty and you have not told her yet. So how old do she got to be, huh? That girl been smart enough to understand a long time ago and you know that, Keith"

"Shut up!" Keith yelled at her. "And do both of us a favor and get out. If I'm gone lose Miracle, it's best that I lose you too. So pack your shit and leave."

Now that's when it hit Sophy that Keith loved Miracle more than he loved her. Now, she wished she had never said nothing to Miracle.

"Keith, where am I going to go?"

"That's not my problem. You'll find a way."

"But I have nowhere to go."

"Sophy, just get your shit and leave."

She walked towards the room then looked back at Keith. He was looking out the front door for Miracle. He had so much concern in his face. Just in the thirty minutes that he been home, he looked like he aged ten years. The stress and the way he felt was unbearable. It brought forward a massive headache and on top of that, he did not spot Miracle anywhere as he looked outside. He wanted to talk to her so badly to at least try and explain to her what things were all about. He hated that Sophy said anything to Miracle about being adopted. Now, what the hell could he do? Adopted or not, Miracle was still his child. He raised her all the way and he was not about to let nothing, or no one come between them. He wanted to make everything right. If not right, he did not want her to hate him.

He wished that he never had told Sophy shit, and he also wished that he would have been told Miracle. He felt all this was his fault for not telling Miracle a long time ago before he even met Sophy. "Damn!" Keith yelled out so loud with so much force that Sophy jumped all the way in the room. She didn't want to be around Keith while he was upset. Keith slammed the front door close with all his might. How could things be going so good one day and it all falls apart the next day. His life has been that way, a big roller coaster. He had been losing his whole life and he was still losing.

Things were moving way too fast for him. He didn't even have enough time to come home and tell his family the good news. At the job meeting, he just got offered a big promotion and a really good raise. He wanted to come home and talk about everything to his family over dinner. What a big surprise he got when he got home. Sophy came out of the room and looked away from Keith. She felt so bad she knew all of this was her fault. She swallowed her pride and made a few trips from the house to her car until she had all her stuff packed in her car. Keith just looked at her, unable to say anything. The sooner she was out of his sight, the better he would feel.

On her way out the house, she put her house key on the table stand next to the door. She walked out and closed the door behind her. Keith waited ten minutes after Sophy left to call Miracle's phone. No answer. He grabbed his car keys, ran out the house, jumped into his car and went looking for her.

Chapter 16

"Welcome to McDonalds. Can I take your order?" Betty said to Tony through the drive through speaker. She'd been working there two months after she got out of prison. She also had a nice studio apartment and she loved going to church. She felt so good, and she even looked good. She kept her weight and her health up. Tony ordered and drove around to the window to pay. He was greeted with a big smile from Betty.

"You look happy today," he told her while he paid for his food.

"Yes I am sir and I give all thanks to God."

She gave him his change and he drove to the next window for his food. He loved the weekends because those were his days off. So many years had passed, and he grown to like his job. He'd seen so many kids grow up and move away. And he also seen so many drop out of school and start hanging on streets corners or on the news. Working for the school really drives a man crazy. Kids all day and then he had two kids of his own. He had to enjoy every moment that he could get alone.

He drove around town just sightseeing while he ate his food. He slammed on brakes and spilled his drink when he saw Tiffany crossing the street. *Why in the hell is this girl walking?* He asked himself out loud. Since he was in a good mood, he decided that he would give her a ride. Plus, he wanted to say hello. As he pulled up on her, he blew the horn. She turned to face him to see who the hell he was. Soon as he saw her face, he said damn this girl has not aged one bit. She still looks exactly the same after all these years. He pulled up on the side of her and let his window down and realized oh shit, this is not Tiffany. She bent down and looked into the car window.

"I'm sorry ma'am, I thought you were someone else."

"Mr. Tony, how are you doing?"

Once she said that, the memory of Miracle riding on his bus came rushing back to his mind.

"Hey, I'm fine now. I remember you. Do you need a ride?"

"Yes please."

"Okay well get in."

Miracle got into the car and put her bag on the backseat.

"So, where are you going?"

"To the airport."

"What! Do you even know how far that is from here?"

"No sir, not really."

"You mean to tell me that you were about to walk all the way there?"

"Yes."

"Well, you had a very long walk ahead of you. But I'll be more than happy to give you a ride."

Tony looked at Miracle and could not believe how much this little girl looked like Tiffany. He could not get that out of his mind.

"So, how is school going?"

"It is okay, I cannot really complain."

"So do you graduate high school this year?"

"No way, Mr. Tony, I'm on my second year in college. I been graduated high school a little while ago."

"College!"

"I remember you riding on my bus. It have not been that long ago."

"Well, I got moved up a couple grades so that pushed me through a little faster. I'm trying to do the same thing in college. I got a few more tests to take, and then I'll see what my placement will be."

Tony had no idea that this little girl was his daughter, and Miracle had no idea that Tony was her real father. They rode the rest of the way in silence. Both of them with thoughts of their own. stuck with their own problems. Tony dropped her off at the airport and told her to be safe. He could not believe how much she looked like Tiffany Tyler as he said goodbye. Plus, her second year in college at that young age. That was outstanding and any parents dream for their child. Miracle boarded her flight and thought about how lost she was. "Damn!" She said out loud. She didn't know who her parents were. Where she was from or who in the hell she was some kin too? She disliked Keith so much right now. How could he not tell her anything? Out of all this time, she thought Gina and Keith were her parents.

She sat on the airplane not sure of what she was about to do. The place she was going she had never been. She felt since she was lost in thought that she might as well start over. North Carolina offered great medical degrees. Miracle bank account rolled over now that she was eighteen. So she was in full control of her money. The state of mind that she was in caused her not to think straight. Keith called her phone many times and every time, he left a voice message. He also texted many times. She ignored all his calls and texts. She felt like he did not care. If he did care, then he would have told her a long time ago.

Out of all these years, now he wants to talk to her about it. She did not trust him. But damn, she loved him so much. In her heart, he was not her father, only a friend. She could never overlook the time he spent with her and the things that he taught her. She was so happy that he did. Because that is what made her up to this point. Keith made sure that she would never give up. Now she were running from her past, which was crazy because that was the only way she would find out the truth. Only Keith could stop the storm inside her head. She just wanted to get some sleep. She did not want to eat. She just wanted to rest. When her flight landed, she caught a taxi to a nice motel and rented a room for seven days. She entered the room and went straight to sleep. After she woke up many hours later, she felt so much better. She washed up and decided to call Keith back to see what he wanted so bad.

"Hello Miracle, we really need to talk," Keith said excitedly into the phone.

"Okay Keith, I'm listening, so talk."

"No, no like this. Where are you so we can talk face to face?"

"Well, Keith!"

"Will you stop saying my name like that? I know you are very upset. But please give me a chance, Miracle."

"Why should I?"

"Because I love you and I'm so sorry, okay."

Miracle felt so bad hearing the cry in Keith's voice. She knew that he loved her and wanted only the best for her.

"Okay Keith, you win. I'm in North Carolina at the Aladdin Motel."

"North Carolina!" Keith yelled "Are you for real?"

"Yes I am."

"Well I'm about to call and book you the first flight back to Florida."

Miracle's flight left at 10:30pm that night. As she flew back home, she knew she had already forgave Keith. But she still wanted him to explain everything to her.

Keith was there to pick her up when her flight landed. When she saw him for some reason, she was too shy to speak. Like a little girl, she felt she was in the wrong. But Keith made the mood so much better with a smile and nice hug.

"Oh Miracle, I missed you so much. Are you okay?"

"Yes, I'm okay, just hungry."

"Well let's go get breakfast," Keith said and grabbed Miracle's bag.

After she ate a few bites of food, she could not hold it in anymore. "So when are you going to tell me what I want to know?"

Keith cleared his throat then said. "First, let me tell you that Gina." He paused and took a deep breath. Just by hearing his voice saying Gina's name out loud touched his heart.

"Well Gina was born with a strange condition that stopped her from ever having kids. But she wanted kids so bad. She used to talk to me about adopting but all I did was push it off. Until one day, she just got fed up with me pushing it off and said Keith today is the day. We went and looked and once she saw you, her mind was made up."

"Who are my real parents, Keith?"

"Miracle, I'm sorry but I do not know. All that was told to us is that you were left on a 7-Eleven store counter the same day you were born by a white lady. You also had a bump on your head. Being that you were saved, they name you Miracle."

"So how in the hell is my mom white?" Miracle said while looking at her skin.

"Your mom can not be white."

"You just said I was left on the store counter by a white lady."

"Yeah but she can't be your mom. We got all your test records. So we know you are black. Maybe the white lady helped your mom birth you. I know I was wrong for not telling you these things sooner. But the truth is, I did not know how to tell you. I tried to protect from hurt all your life. Until I ended up being the one that hurt you the most. I tried to prepare the right time to tell you. Miracle, please forgive me and let's move together as a family. You are all I have, and you are all I love. So give me another chance."

"Keith I'll forgive you and give you another chance only if you promise me one thing."

"I'll do anything for you, Miracle."

"I want to find them and ask them why." Tears rolled down Miracle's cute little face.

Keith got up and hugged her. "It's okay, I will help you find them."

He just held her for a little while to calm her down.

Tiffany's health got so bad that her doctor upgraded her medication to max. She felt so weak and the pain in her side started to come more. Her job placed her on light duty. She called her parents and told them about her condition and wanted to know if she could move back home. That she needed help to take care of herself it was too much to live alone. She needed more rest, and she could not do that and still provide for herself. She also needed a donor real soon. Her parents said yes that they would love to have her back home. And that they do not want her to stress and that they would help her in any way they could. They all decided for her to move back next month. No matter her age or condition, they loved her as they did when she was a baby. They were well off with money. So to help take care of their daughter was no problem. By all means they wanted her back home. They both were up in age and needed something to do. They talked on the phone for a while then they all prayed before hanging up.

Betty had become a member at the same church Miracle went to. She was the third white person in the church. But she felt the love of the church. The church was wonderful, and the message of God was so strong. They embraced Betty as soon as she walked in. Color was not an issue. Betty joined the prayer and worship group. On Betty's special day, Miracle, Keith or Sophy were not present. Betty stood in the middle of the church and gave testimony. From how she had kids she has not seen in years. To how she got strung out on drugs, lost everything and became a bum. All the way until she found that little baby in the dumpster. She felt that was her turning point. She asked to be forgiving for leaving that little baby on that store counter and to be reunited with her kids. The church prayed with her and for her. The church thanked her for her open testimony. Betty felt so much better that she let all that out. Now her heart was clear, and she could start over. She knew she was on her way to a better life. Now, she fully understands that in life it's not just about love. It's about the value of what you love the most.

Chapter 17

After Miracle passed the national medical board, she was called to work in Providence. Her performance were great as she built a name for herself. She did not like the fact that she had to move far away from home but she had to take the opportunity. Providence was the only place that offered her a job full time. They were in dying need of a surgeon. Her first patient was a nine year old Spanish boy who was born with infected kidney's due to his mom doing drugs while she was pregnant with him. He was a very bright kid that spoke no English. His name was Kevin. He had dark brown hair and had a smile that would melt our hearts. DCF took him from his parents at birth. Once they found out about all the drugs that were in his mom's system when she gave birth, they recommended to have his mom arrested. His uncle took custody of him when he were born to keep him with the family. Since he were a kid, he were placed first on the donor list. His uncle and his uncle's wife were both unhappy to see Miracle as his surgeon. They saw how young she were and did not like that. Plus once they found out that Kevin would be her first patient, they tried to back out to get another surgeon. The doctor informed them that Miracle is certified and that she will perform the surgery and that it was no other surgeon within twenty seven hundred miles that could perform this type of surgery. Plus, they told them that Miracle was the only surgeon under their contract. So if they wanted another surgeon, they would have to go to another hospital. And that Kevin's body are not strong enough to be moved around. Also, that he needed to go into surgery within the next two hours if they wanted him to have a fighting chance. Besides, Miracle would end up being his surgeon anyway on this coast. They both gave in and let Miracle do her job.

"Hello, I'm Doctor Marshall," Miracle said as she stuck out her hand to introduce herself. "Are you Kevin's two parents?"

Before they greeted or spoke to Miracle, the uncle's wife asked her.

"How old are you?"

"I'm twenty three," Miracle said with a nice smile.

"Oh my God, she is still a baby," The uncle's wife yelled out.

Miracle looked down at the ground. She felt odd but she knew she had to get these people to believe in her. She lifted up her head and said,

"Mrs. and Mr., the surgery that Kevin needs is not that difficult. All the blood work matches up with the donor's parts. It do not matter if Kevin is my first patient or not. I will perform on him as I will my own child. I know how hard it is for the both of you but I have sixteen years of experience. I have passed tests most surgeons can't till this day."

"Ma'am, you said you have sixteen years of experience. How is that when you are only twenty three?"

101

Their English was not that good, so Miracle really had to listen.

"Yes it's crazy but I have been doing this since I was seven years old."

That made them both laugh a little.

Miracle stuck her hand back out and said, "Trust me please."

The uncle shook her hand.

Miracle said, "Thank you," and turned to leave.

The surgery went great for Miracle. She could not believe it herself. To her it was simple and fast. Even though she took her time to make sure she did everything right and complete. Once Miracle gave the great news to Kevin's uncle and his wife, they could not stop thanking her. She could understand their happiness because she felt good herself. She felt like she was floating for a moment. What brightened her day even more was when Keith and Dr. Wheelin, who retired two years ago with a perfect record of never losing a patient, showed up. She had no idea that they were there. At first, she could not believe her eyes.

"So I take it that it all went well by the way you are smiling," Keith said.

"Yes! Yes!" Miracle said out of excitement. I had no idea that you two were here.

"Are you crazy? We would not miss this moment for nothing."

"This is your first step; your first test and we are here for you now and always. I was even willing to come back there and help you if you needed help."

"That is so nice of you, Dr. Wheelin. Well, how about we all celebrate tonight?"

"I think that is a great idea," Keith and Dr. Wheelin said.

Miracle felt so special. She was so overjoyed that she forgot about Kevin's family for a few minutes.

"I'll see you guys later tonight," she said and walked back over to Kevin's family.

"I'm sorry about that. But my dad wanted to make sure the surgery went well."

She studied her chart then told them that she has to run some more tests on Kevin, and then he will be moved downstairs.

"Please do know that he needs plenty of rest. His body is still a little weak. Right now he is still under medication. So he is sleep. I'm going to allow the both of you to see him for a short period of time. But please do not try to wake him. Once the medication wears off, he will awake on his own. And no hugs. His body is very sore. Any questions?"

"No, and thank you, young lady," The uncle's wife said.

Tiffany Tyler was doing good when she first moved back in with her parents. But now, her health had become a major factor. Her kidney failure was so bad that it caused strain to her liver. She needed a donor more sooner than later. Her weight was dropping, and the pills did not get rid of the pain any more. The doctor did not want her on all kinds of medication because it tears down the liver. She went back to the same church. No matter how bad she felt, she still went to church. The doctor told her that her blood type was hard to find. So she knew it was a chance that she were not going to find a donor. Her blood type was O negative. And she was still seven years back on the donor list. The church gave Tiffany and her family all the support they could, but they all faced the fact that she would not make it. But their faith kept them all strong. Keith felt so bad for Tiffany. He did not tell Miracle about it. He did not want to stress her. She was doing so good in Providence and had received many awards from the medical board. She was the second surgeon in the U.S. that could perform any type of surgery. She was already upset by having no luck in finding her parents. Keith stayed on the path for her to find out something. But all the roads keep leading to a dead end. Through the years that had passed Keith and Miracle have contacted so many people and agencies. They even hired a private investigator that came back with no leads. He still could hear Miracle frustrated words.

I didn't just drop out of the sky.

"Now that he thought about it to himself, maybe you did," he said out loud. He decided to wait until Miracle came back to town to tell her about her friend Tiffany. That way they could both go visit her together. No one knew the stress Tiffany had and no one knew that she was sneaking out at twelve midnight to go to the bar and drink.

As Keith sat home thinking to himself, he heard a knock on the front door. He opened the door to see Sophy standing there with a little boy. He has not seen or heard from her since that day he kicked her out and he wished she were not here now. She didn't even work at the college anymore.

"Can I help you?" He asked her.

"I don't want anything from you, Keith. I just want you and your son to meet each other."

"My son!" Keith felt like he went deaf for a few seconds.

He could not believe Sophy's words. The little boy was looking up at him with eyes just like his.

"Say hello to your daddy, Little Keith."

"Hi, daddy," the little boy said.

Keith dropped down on both knees in front of his son. "What's your name, lil man?"

He looked up at his mom then looked back at Keith and said, "Keith Marshall Jr."

He squeezed his mom's hand to show that he was shy of Keith. Keith looked up at Sophy.

"Is this really my son?"

"Yes and we will be leaving now."

"No!" Keith yelled as he stood up. "Wait come in for a little while. We need to talk."

As he looked at Sophy, he noticed that she had a wedding ring on. And he knew that Sophy could be full of shit. His stare at the ring was so noticeable.

She said, "I could not afford to raise him by myself."

"Will you come in please?"

They both stepped in and sat down.

"So, how old is he?"

"Four years young."

"Why you did not contact me, Sophy?"

"Because I hated you Keith. You kicked me out with no place to go. I had to use all my savings to get a place. Then, I found out I was pregnant. At first, I wanted to get an abortion but I stayed strong and fought against that. I did not want to see you again, so I transferred schools. Now I do admit that it was stupid and childish of me to use our child against you, but I realize it did not hurt you because you did not know about our child. Keith, I was so mad at you that I did not want you to be a part of our lives. But my husband talked me into forgiving you. I had to agree with the advice that he gave me. He told me that if I really do love my son, then forgive his father. Plus, I know that holding secrets will break a child down like it did Miracle. I'm also willing to give you a blood test to prove that he is your son. I also want to tell you sorry twice. One for my wrongdoing by telling Miracle what I had no business telling her. And second, for keeping you out of your son's life these four years. I also want to apologize to Miracle. Also Keith, by me being selfish, I ask you not to take that out on our child. I want him to know you and love you just as much as he does me."

"I understand, Sophy, and I'm just so mind blown right now. About this child and about how much you done changed."

"If you need a little time Keith to take this all in, I can respect that."

"No it's not that. I'm just so happy right now. This is more than great news."

"So when do you want to take the blood test?"

"Anytime you are ready, Sophy." Keith could look at the lil boy and tell that it was his child.

"I'll set it for next week. Here is my card if you want to contact me. Well, me and Lil Keith have to be going now."

"So, when can I get him?"

"Just call me Keith."

Tony was at the bar twelve thirty in the morning still drinking. He tried to drink his problems away. The more he thought about it, the more he drank. He could not close his eyes. When he did, the sight kept coming back to him. He loved his family and maybe that was the problem. He loved them too much. But how dare his wife out of all these years try him like that. Hard as he worked all these years to be the provider for his family. Today, he came home from work early to see a strange car in his driveway. He walked into his house to see his wife bent over the living room sofa from the back getting pounded by a white guy.

What the hell did I do wrong? He yelled out loud at the top of his lungs as his anger built up. The people in the bar looked his way and knew that he was going through it. By the way he reacted once he saw his wife, he knew he went too far. But what man would not react out of his feelings put in that situation? Was he about to go to jail? He did not know and at this point, he did not care. All he wanted was a good life.

107

Both of his kids were grown and out on their own. As he thought back on the events that took place when he walked in on his wife, the white guy saw him first but could not react fast enough. Tony football tackled the guy to the ground. Never in his life have he ever fought a naked man. Somehow, the guy rolled on top of him but the guy just seemed too slow and too weak to contain Tony. Tony threw the white guy off him. Then, got on top of the guy and started punching him in the face with all his might, and to his surprise his wife bust him in the head with a flower vase.

That hit knocked him over and caused the white guy to get on top of him and start to choke him. The white guy was not hurting him at all. While down on the ground, he looked his wife in the eye to make sure that she knew it was him. He thought that she could not know that it was him. But once they locked eyes and she told him to get out, he lost all control at that moment. Because for her to turn on him like that told him it was no love.

Tony elbowed the white guy in the nose as hard as he could. The white guy tumbled over and rolled on his back holding his nose with his legs open. Tony jumped up and kicked him in his groin as hard as he could. They guy took a deep breath and passed out. His wife screamed then she charged at him with her head down. Tony uppercut her as soon as she got close enough. She dropped to the floor like she had been head shotted.

Both of them being unconscious, he went into the bedroom, got another set of clothes and took the safe that he kept under the bed. Then, he decided to leave. On his way out the door, he stopped and took the house key off his key chain and threw it on the floor next to his wife. He slammed the front door and left. As he drove, he took his bloody shirt off and cleaned his face and head with the clean part. He wanted to turn around and go back to fight some more. All these years passed, and he never hit his wife and not one time did she hit him. So, why did she react like that? She did not say sorry or act shocked when she saw him. He drove and cried like a little kid. He never even cheated on his wife. He turned his back on Tiffany Tyler a long time ago for her.

"Oh God!" He yelled out loud. A name that he never called on before. As he drove, he spotted the bar and decided that is what he needed a stiff drink. The more he thought about it as he sat at the bar, the more he drank. It was daylight outside when he walked into the bar. He had no idea that it was dark outside or how long he had been in the bar. All he wanted was drink after drink.

Tiffany Tyler sat in the back of the bar at her personal table watching Tony. She was waiting on him to leave. She did not want to be seen and especially not by Tony. As she watched him, she could see that he was drinking way too much. Tony sat at the bar on the stool drinking shot after shot. She wished so bad that he would stop and just go home. She knew he had gotten too drunk to drive. She disliked him, but she still cared for him as a person. For some strange reason, she felt that they both were cursed for the death of that little baby a long time ago. She just kept her eyes on Tony. Her first love and only love. She saw Tony fall straight off the stool and hit the floor. He passed out from drinking too much. The people in the little bar rushed to help him. The owner of the bar started freaking out.

"I'm calling the cops," he said and picked up the phone.

"He's okay. He just had a little too much to drink. Give him a little time and he will be okay." A guy that was bent over Tony told the owner.

Tiffany knew Tony worked for the schoolboard and did not want him to lose his job by drinking.

"He's a good friend of mine, " she said as she jumped up and walked towards the crowd.

The owner of the bar looked at Tiffany. He knew she came in the bar at late hours and never spoke or even bothered anyone.

"Please do not call the cops. He is a great friend of mine. I'll take care of him from here."

"Well okay," the bar owner said.

He hung up the phone and said, "Get him out of here."

"We all will help you get him in the car, ma'am." Three of the guys said as they lifted Tony off the ground and followed Tiffany outside to her car.

She opened the passenger side door and laid the seat all the way back so Tony could lay back in the car. They put Tony in the car. Then asked, if she wanted them to follow her home to help get him out.

"No thanks guys. I got it from here and thank you all for the help."

Tiffany got into the car and let the windows down so some fresh air could get rid of the loud liquor smell that was coming off of Tony. She knew she could not take him to her parents' house. She also knew that she could not take him home to his wife. Not at this type of hour. His wife knew of their relationship a long time ago. So it was no telling how his wife would act if she pulled up with Tony drunk like this. So, she decided to drive to the beach and park. Maybe the fresh air and sound of the water will help sober Tony up. As they sat there, all she could do was stare at him and just wonder what was wrong with him. She never knew him to be a drinker. She looked him up and down and so many memories came rushing back to her of them. Some bad but most good, if not great. At that moment, she realized that she still loved him. She was thinking what the hell was she going to tell him that would convince him that she just bumped into him. She did not want him to know that she was in the bar. Then, she fought back her shyness and would be who she was. That is one reason why she missed out on a lot in her life. By trying to please Tony. So now she will have her chance to tell him how she really feel and how she felt. All these years that passed, she found herself blaming Tony for everything that went wrong in her life since he left her for the worst.

Chapter 18

Miracle could not believe her eyes. The papers that Keith showed her said. 99.9 percent that he was the father of Lil Keith. Miracle still had a big dislike for Sophy but the little boy was so cute and for some reason, he clung to Miracle. Lil Keith was so quiet and sweet but not shy. Sophy let him spend the weekends with Keith so they could start a relationship. Lil Keith was crazy about his Miami Dolphins football. He took it everywhere he went and if you tried to take it, he would cry his lil heart out. He had just met Miracle and he followed her everywhere.

"So, how long are you staying, Miracle?" Keith asked her.

"I really do not know at this point. I might be staying for good this time."

"Why you say that? Are you going to be on call or something?"

"No Keith, I did not want to tell anyone but I lost my first patient. So to make sure that will be my last, I'm planning on giving it up."

"No way. I cannot accept that kind of talk from you."

"Well I'm telling you now. Because I do not ever want to go through anything like that again."

"But you know that is part of your job, right?"

"Keith, have you ever had to look a child's parents in the eyes and tell them that their child is dead? Do you know that part is harder than losing the patient? Keith, I tried my best and my best was not good enough. That little girl's body was so weak that her chance of dying was greater than her chance of living. But her family believed in me more than they believed in God, and that is what most people do not understand that the decision is up to God if the patient lives or dies. I'm human, I only perform procedures.

As Miracle talked, she started shaking and crying. Keith gave her a tight hug. Even Lil Keith felt Miracle's pain. He started crying just because he saw her crying. Seeing that little boy cry for her cheered her up. She forced herself to laugh so Lil Keith would know she was okay. Keith did not want to tell her about her friend Tiffany, but he did not want to hold any more secrets over her head.

"Miracle, I got some bad news for you about your friend, Tiffany."

"Is she okay?"

"Yes for now, she is but she really has gotten worse. She really need a donor. You already know that she moved back with her parents. She are getting so weak, and it is starting to show. I hate to be the one to tell you, but she is looking like she is giving up. That happy jolly look she don't carry that around anymore. I think it will be a great idea if you pay her a visit. It's been a long time since you two saw each other. It should bring a nice smile to her face to see you."

"I'll plan to go see her Keith, but I still have my own problems. And it is really stressing me that I can't find my parents. All the money we both have spent trying to come up with something is crazy. I never thought it would be this hard. I don't hate my parents; I just want to ask them why."

"Miracle, I feel your pain, but I am your family. No matter what happens you got me and Lil Keith. So how about you giving me and Lil Keith some of that good cooking?"

Miracle laughed and looked at Lil Keith who looked like he was sleepy.

"Okay, I can do that for you two."

Miracle cooked yellow rice, fried chicken, cut green beans and sweet corn bread. Miracle and Keith both watched Lil Keith as they all ate. Keith still could not believe he had a son. It still was so mind blowing to him. He wanted full custody of his son. Even though he knew it would not happen, no matter what Sophy said he could not just forgive her for holding this lil boy out of his life for four years. But to stay in his child's life, he had to hold all that anger in. He knew Sophy could be a real nasty bitch. So it was in his best interest not to piss her off. He was more than happy to have Miracle back home. But he could not just let her give up. She worked too hard all her lil life just to let it all go. After dinner, they all washed up and went to bed.

"Well, hello there," Tiffany said to Tony soon as his eyes opened.

Tony blinked his eyes repeatedly trying to make sure he was seeing correctly.

"What the hell is going on?" He said as he looked around. Not knowing how he got where he was or how he got with Tiffany.

Tiffany, not liking his attitude, spoke out in anger.

"Instead of complaining Tony, how about saying thank you? The owner in the bar was going to call the cops on you for falling out in his bar. But I stepped up and told him that you are a good friend of mine and that I will take care of you. I did not want you to go to jail and lose your job, and I did not want to take you home to your wife in the middle of the morning. It's no telling what your wife would say or think. So that is why we are here. I parked until you came too."

All at once, everything that happened that night came back rushing to him. His head pounded like crazy as his blood started to boil. Then, he looked at Tiffany clearly for the first time.

"I think I might be going to jail anyway, Tiffany."

"What, why?" She asked.

He told her everything that happened with his wife. Tiffany felt bad for him and did not want him to go to jail.

"Tony, you cannot drink your problems away. I'm so sorry to hear about that. It really is bad. Not to add to your problems, Tony but I have some things I want to talk to you about that I have been dealing with."

"Go ahead, Tiffany. My life is at an end anyway."

"Well first off, the last time we were together you called me a murderer and that have been stuck in my head all these years. Do you even know what I went through to please you? I gave up everything for you, Tony. I slept house to house. Some nights I did not eat or shower because I love you. I protected you from going to jail for fucking with a minor, and now look I'm still protecting you from going to jail now. Twenty some years later, Tony. I gave up my one and only child by chasing you. Not only that, but I'm also suffering from kidney failure. My health is not one hundred percent. All I wanted was to be with you. So please tell me, Tony, what did I do wrong?"

Tears rolled down Tiffany's face uncontrollably.

"I don't know what to tell you, Tiffany."

"How about the truth, Tony.

"Okay first off, you were too young, and I was not in love with you. I was just having sex with you and the thought of you getting pregnant never crossed my mind until it happened. I did not want a relationship with you."

"So, why did you tell me you love me?" She asked Tony.

"Because that is what you wanted to hear."

Tiffany turned her head away from Tony and looked out the driver side window. The sight of Tony was now making her sick. She could not hold back the cry sounds anymore. She cried and she cried hard. Tony just sat there and watched her. He did not want to touch her or say anything. He touched her shoulder then pulled her to him. He held her and told her now as a man that he apologize.

"I was young also, Tiffany, so I made stupid choices also. What you did not know is that through all these years I have been hurting also. For not helping you and telling you I'm sorry. I want you to forgive me, and I want to tell you that I forgive you about the baby. We both were too young at that time but let's make our days to come better."

She stopped crying. She never thought that he felt any type of way. His words sounded so good.

"I'm very sorry, Tiffany, for hurting you and leaving you all alone. Yes, I was less than a man. To be honest, I am so happy to be with you right now. I'm not selfish, Tiffany but I am broken right now. I have no idea on how my life is going to end up. I don't want to fight anymore. I just want to be happy."

"I forgive you, Tony. I never knew you felt the way you do. I do not want to be sad anymore or to dislike you. I'm happy that we both got this chance to talk this out. Now that we have all that behind us, where do you want me to drop you off at? Because I'm tired."

"Just take me back to my car."

Chapter 19

Keith talked Miracle into going back to work and not giving up. She decided to stay local so she could be close to home while her and Keith still searched for her parents. Her and Lil Keith got along so well that it made her think about having kids. She knew it was about time that she started dating. Even Tiffany Tyler had a boyfriend now. When Tiffany first brought Tony, the bus driver to church, Miracle thought it was so funny. She did not know that they were a couple. Tiffany was so happy with Tony. They even came over once a month to eat with Keith and Miracle. Church were good and everyone had love for each other. Miracle and Lil Keith were more than brother and sister, they were best friends.

The days were great until Miracle got a call on her business phone. She was needed at once. All she could say is I'm on my way. As soon as she got to the hospital, they handed her the chart.

An older couple stopped her from reading it.

"Doctor, can you please help our daughter? She is all we have. We do not have a lot of money but you can have everything we own."

The mother grabbed Miracle's hand and led her to their daughter's room. Miracle hated this feeling; it made her think back to the time she lost a patient.

"She's been sick for a while," the mother said, then stepped into the room.

Miracle whole heart dropped when she saw Tiffany Tyler laying in that bed. Her mind went completely blank.

"Hey Miracle, I recommended you," Tiffany said with a smile.

For the first time, Miracle looked and read the medical chart in her hands. She looked up at Tiffany's parents and said, "She do not have a donor."

"We know but we pray she gets one soon."

Miracle turned to the other doctor and asked a bunch of questions while she read the medical file again. Miracle could not believe that it was Tiffany laying in this bed. She never worked on someone she knew before. She was told that Tiffany needed a donor within seventy two hours, and Miracle knew without a shadow of a doubt that she was not going to get one. So, now she was stuck telling her best friend that she would not make it. What was even harder than that was to tell Tiffany's parents that there was nothing she could do to save their daughter. That Tiffany needs a donor more than she needs a doctor.

"Hey there, how are you doing?" Miracle asked Tiffany.

"I need you to save me, Miracle. I have heard so much about how good you are. So, please help me. I'll give you all I have."

"I'm sorry Tiffany, but there's nothing I can do for you without a donor. That's the bad news I have for you all. You have to get a donor like now. If not, then you will not make it no more than seventy two hours."

"So even if I'm on the verge of death, I still have to wait on the donor list."

"It's the way the system is run."

"So, do you think I will get a donor in time?" Tiffany asked out of fear Miracle heard it in her voice.

Miracle could not look Tiffany in the face and answer that. She just walked out of the room into the hallway. She saw the female pastor and Betty from her church. They were looking for Miracle's room. As soon as they both spotted Miracle crying they ran up to her.

"Are you okay?" Betty asked.

"No it's Tiffany. I cannot stand to see her like that, and I cannot help her without a donor. She only has hours left to live."

"Oh my God!" The pastor yelled out. "Come on, let's all go pray for her."

All three of them walked into Tiffany's room. Bad as she felt, she still smiled as soon as she saw them. Her parents walked out the room to give Tiffany some time with her friends. They all took turns hugging Tiffany and they all cried.

"Okay y'all, let's pray," the pastor said. "Tiffany, is there anything you want to confess first so that you will be forgiven for all sins?"

Tiffany thought about it for a while and then said yes it is. I don't want you all to judge me. Please just hear me out. When I was young, I committed murder and never got caught. All the women looked at each other wide eyes. I was young, like sixteen. I gave birth to a little baby girl one night on my own with no hospital. To stay with the baby daddy, I threw my baby away in a trash dumpster. Betty's ears started to burn as she listened. I was so stupid and when I went back to that dumpster to get my baby the next day, it was empty. The garbage truck had dumped it. I never saw my lil girl again. That's how she died."

Wait a minute, Tiffany," Betty spoke up. "Are you talking about The Green Apartments over twenty years ago?"

"Yes, how do you know that?"

"Because I was there. I used to be a bum and I stayed behind that dumpster, and that night I got that little baby out of that dumpster."

Tiffany lost her breath at first. Then, she said are you serious? What did you do with my baby?"

"I took that lil baby to the 7-eleven store and left her on the store counter.

Miracle swallowed her spit. Her mouth was extra dry. Because Keith told her that is the way she was found. Miracle asked to be excused. She left the room and went straight to the blood lab. She found Tiffany Tyler's blood and tested both of their blood to see if Tiffany was her mom. The results knocked her to her knees. All this time her mom had been right in her face. She stood back up and did more blood comparisons. Then, she made a call to Dr. Wheelin. She was still stuck in her thoughts. But now she knew that Tiffany was her mom. Should she forgive Tiffany for throwing her away? Maybe Tiffany did not deserve to know that her daughter was alive or who her daughter was. Much hate as Miracle felt, it was just not in her to tell Tiffany the truth. At least she could let her mom die in peace. As she thought about it, she went back over her work twice to make sure she was correct. Then, she knew right then what to do. She got down on her knees and prayed. She asked for strength to forgive her mom and for her to be forgiving from the hate she felt. Now, she could find out who her father was. Miracle walked back to Tiffany's room to find a crowded room full of people praying. Tiffany's parents and Tony were in the room. Just by seeing all of them together praying made Miracle's heart ache for Tiffany, or should she says her mom? Dr. Wheelin showed up at once when Miracle said it's an emergency.

She explained everything to him then they called Keith to tell him and to see what he thought about it and how he felt, even though Miracle already had her mind made up. When Keith arrived, they still talked about it. Keith was blown away by the fact that Tiffany was Miracle's mom. They all went over the test results, and it was clear to see that Miracle was right. Miracle was so excited by finding her mom that she told Keith the story she heard twice. Everything added up to how she was left on that counter.

"So when are you going to tell her, before or after the surgery?" Keith asked Miracle.

"That's the part I'm thinking so hard about."

"Well if you want my advice, I say tell her before. In case anything goes wrong, she would have known the truth."

"Yeah, you are right, Keith. But I'm gone wait until after."

Dr. Wheelin stepped in and said, "Well, if we are going to save her, the sooner the better.

Can we go over everything again please? I'm nervous," Miracle said.

Everything matched up and Miracle was more than healthy enough to donate her kidney. Miracle forgave Tiffany and decided to donate her kidney to save her mom's life. It was a big decision that she thought of all on her own. She loved Tiffany enough to forgive her. She called Dr. Wheelin to perform the surgeries on them. He agreed just like she thought he would. And now all the talk about it was over. It was time to get it over with. The longer they waited, the less chance Tiffany had of making it.

"I'm ready," Miracle said. "But I do not want her to know that I'm the donor yet. You can tell her whenever you please. Dr. Wheelin went to Tiffany's room and told them that she has a donor, and the surgery needs to be done now.

They all clapped and thanked God.

"Our prayers have been answered!" The pastor yelled out.

"Where is Miracle?" Tiffany asked.

She's waiting for you in the other room so let's go, everything is already set. Tiffany was so happy that she did not ask who the donor was, and really she did care. Dr. Wheelin loved Miracle not just as a friend but as a goddaughter also. He admired her decision to donate a kidney to Tiffany. That was a bold choice, and it took a strong woman to do so. Dr. Wheelin performed his best every time, and right now he did his best. The surgeries went well. Once they were done, they were placed in separate rooms as Miracle requested.

Chapter 20

The next day, Miracle got all her papers and went to Tiffany's room. She fought back the pain. Sore as she was, she did not care. She just wanted answers. She could not hold the urge back any more. Tiffany parents and Tony, the bus driver, were in her room when Miracle walked in.

"Hello everyone."

They all looked at her as if she were a ghost. Being that she was in a hospital gown. Then, they all spoke to her one by one.

"Can I have a private talk with Tiffany please?"

"Yes," Tiffany's mom said and jumped up.

"But first, we want to thank you for saving her. You did a great job with the surgery." Miracle forced a smile while they walked out.

"Miracle, thank you for saving me, and why are you dressed in that hospital gown?"

"We will get to that later. I want to talk to you about your daughter."

"Hey before you say anything else. Miracle my daughter is alive somewhere."

"Yes, I know she is alive. I'm your daughter."

"You're what," Tiffany said and sat up in her bed.

"I have these papers to prove it to you." Miracle handed her the papers.

"I was adopted and the night I was born, I was left on the 7-Eleven store counter, and I did the blood test on us. It's a complete match."

Tiffany could not speak. She just cried as she read the paperwork. She really could not believe that this was happening and that it was all true.

"Oh my God. I do not know what to say. But I'm sorry and I'm so happy at the same time."

"Mom or should I say Tiffany. Why did you throw me away?"

Tiffany just sat there for a moment and cried. Then, she spoke.

"Miracle, I was young and so so stupid. Plus, I was in love. I wanted your father so badly that I was blind to everything else. All my life I have been praying to have that moment back. I would never make that mistake again. It's really not too much I can explain to you, Miracle. Besides, I was so stupid. I really do want to put that behind us. So, if you can find it in your heart, please forgive me."

Miracle looked up to the ceiling with tears rolling down her face.

"That's why you are alive mom. Because I already forgave you. I gave you one of my kidneys to save you. That is why I'm dressed in this hospital gown. I valued your love and your need to live over anything else in this world. Even over myself."

"So, you're my donor?"

"Yes!"

"You sacrificed your whole life for me? Miracle, all I can say is thank you from the bottom of my heart, and that I promise you if you give me the chance, I'm going to be the best mom I can be."

"So, tell me, who my father is?"

"Tony," she said pointing to the door he just left out of.

"Tony, the bus driver!"

"Yes, how do you know he drives the school bus?"

"Mom, I rode on his bus for school."

"Wow, now I see why they say it's a small world."

"Call all of them back in so we can talk."

They all came back into the room.

"Hey, you all," Tiffany spoke with so much excitement in her voice. "I have great news. Tony, this is our daughter that we both thought was dead. And mom and dad, this is your granddaughter."

Tony rushed Miracle and picked her up off the floor.

"I knew you and Tiffany looked so much alike."

He hugged her and Miracle hugged him back.

"Oh my, I'm so happy. I never got the chance to hold you so I'm holding you now," he said then he put her down.

"We really have a granddaughter?" Tiffany's mom said.

"I also want to tell you all that she is also my donor. She saved my life. And I'm still blown by the steps she took to save me. Miracle, I owe you everything. I wish I could share with you this joy I'm feeling. It's so much at one time. It's like the ultimate high of life. I prayed for this day. But it's way better than what I prayed for, and I still can't believe it is true. If this is a dream, I don't ever want to wake up. I know now that we all value things in life and most of the things are not worth it, but the value of love is what life is all about. I thank God that you are alive and now a part of all our lives. So, please all of us, let's pray."

The End.

Made in United States
Orlando, FL
03 March 2023

30639427R00072